"Hello?" Henry answered, putting the call on Speaker.

"You were warned there would be consequences," the voice on the other end said. Though it was more of a distorted hodgepodge of recorded words and syllables—both male and female, a variety of ages and accents—spliced together and spouted through some fancy software.

Allison and Henry shared a glance. "Please don't hurt our son," she begged.

"Reveal the new identities and locations of the three witnesses who have testified against Los Chacales at the press conference."

Inside, Allison screamed. She couldn't expose the identities of the other marshals in her office, tell the world where they lived. Make them and their families targets. Turn the USMS into a spectacle.

"The choice is yours," Vargas said, hiding behind that damn software.

"Proof of life," Henry blurted as if the thought had just occurred to him. "We want proof our son is alive and unharmed."

"You will get it. Then you'll have until 9:00 a.m. Fail again and there will be more bloodshed."

INNOCENT HOSTAGE

Juno Rushdan

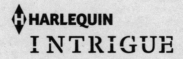

This book is for my husband, who is my best friend and
the ultimate teammate, for all those couples out there who
believe in the power of love, and for every fearless romantic.

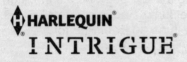

Recycling programs
for this product may
not exist in your area.

ISBN-13: 978-1-335-40174-8

Innocent Hostage

Copyright © 2021 by Juno Rushdan

All rights reserved. No part of this book may be used or reproduced in
any manner whatsoever without written permission except in the case of
brief quotations embodied in critical articles and reviews.

This is a work of fiction. Names, characters, places and incidents
are either the product of the author's imagination or are used fictitiously.
Any resemblance to actual persons, living or dead, businesses,
companies, events or locales is entirely coincidental.

This edition published by arrangement with Harlequin Books S.A.

For questions and comments about the quality of this book,
please contact us at CustomerService@Harlequin.com.

Harlequin Enterprises ULC
22 Adelaide St. West, 40th Floor
Toronto, Ontario M5H 4E3, Canada
www.Harlequin.com

Printed in U.S.A.

Juno Rushdan is the award-winning author of steamy, action-packed romantic thrillers that keep you on the edge of your seat. She writes about kick-ass heroes and strong heroines fighting for their lives as well as their happily-ever-afters. As a veteran air force intelligence officer, she uses her background supporting Special Forces to craft realistic stories that make you sweat and swoon. Juno currently lives in the DC area with her patient husband, two rambunctious kids and a spoiled rescue dog. To receive a FREE book from Juno, sign up for her newsletter at junorushdan.com/mailing-list. Also be sure to follow Juno on BookBub for the latest on sales at bit.ly/BookBubJuno.

Books by Juno Rushdan

Harlequin Intrigue

A Hard Core Justice Thriller

Hostile Pursuit
Witness Security Breach
High-Priority Asset
Innocent Hostage

Visit the Author Profile page at Harlequin.com.

CAST OF CHARACTERS

Allison Chen-Boyd—Separated from her husband, she is going through a contentious divorce, but has never let her personal problems get in the way of doing her job until the unthinkable happens. She is the only deputy marshal linked to the witnesses who testified against the Los Chacales cartel. There's no doubt in her mind the leader of the cartel is behind her son's abduction.

Henry Boyd—FBI Hostage Rescue Team leader. He's still in love with his wife, but he's not sure if they can ever overcome their marital issues. No matter what, he'll do anything to get his son back.

Benjamin Boyd—Allison and Henry's eight-year-old son.

Emilio Vargas—The leader of the deadliest, most powerful drug cartel, Los Chacales. He has a score to settle with the US Marshals and will stop at nothing to achieve vengeance.

Tobias Keogh—Special agent in charge of the San Diego field office and Henry's best friend.

Will Draper—US marshal in charge of the San Diego office.

Kevin Roessler—Police captain and task force liaison.

Chapter One

It was bad enough Allison had to worry about the head of the deadliest, most powerful drug cartel coming after her, but now Henry was trying to steal her son.

After nearly nine years of marriage, she didn't want things to devolve into mudslinging and playing dirty. Benjamin was their son, after all, but he was *her* baby.

The only way Henry would get full custody, uprooting Ben from San Diego and dragging him across the country to Quantico, Virginia, was over her dead body. Though she was more inclined to kill Henry. She was consumed with outrage and would fight tooth and nail for Ben.

Allison spun the wedding band on her finger, debating for the umpteenth time whether to go through the trouble of changing her last name from Chen-Boyd, dropping Henry's surname. Ben was a Boyd. People assumed she was, too, and it wasn't as if she was ever getting married again. Going through the marital mill once was plenty.

But obliterating the hyphen that formally tied her to Henry seemed a necessary formality. The dissolution of a marriage had to be marked with more than paperwork. Didn't it?

She took off her diamond *eternity* ring—the irony of the term a slap to the face—and tossed it onto the porcelain dish on the nightstand by her side of the bed.

God, she still had a side after six months separated and living apart. Like some desperate part of her brain was holding out hope that, somehow beyond the scope of reality or reason, she and Henry would fix what was broken in their marriage. Find a way to keep their family whole.

She made the bed, silently vowing to sleep spread-eagle right in the center tonight.

Allison put on her suit jacket and hurried down the stairs of her Spanish Colonial home, kicking herself for letting Henry persuade her into buying it rather than the Craftsman she'd loved. She was going to be the one stuck in a Mediterranean-style house she'd never wanted. Maybe she should kick Henry when she saw him in twenty minutes to meet with the mediator.

Violence solves nothing. She had to remind herself of that every time she prepared to see the man who'd once been the love of her life. Who'd broken her heart and left her wounded.

She fastened the latch over her US Marshals Service–issued Glock, securing it to the holster on her hip, before going into the kitchen.

Ben sat on a stool at the counter, devouring pancakes.

Allison kissed his head. "Morning, munchkin."

"Ugh!" Ben pushed her away. "Stop it, Mom." He threw a furtive glance at Tori, the cute redhead who was their part-time nanny while she worked on her degree in child development.

Allison rolled her eyes at her seven-year-old son's crush on the sitter.

Tori smiled. "My mom still kisses me on the head, and she gives the best hugs. I like it, knowing how much she loves me."

Allison dared to kiss Ben again and ruffle his hair. That time he didn't pull away. She looked at Tori and mouthed, *Thank you.*

After grabbing a travel mug, she went for the coffeepot. "I appreciate you swinging by this morning and taking Ben to school. I tried to get a later mediation appointment, but…" She bit her tongue, trying hard not to say anything negative about Henry in front of Ben. If Henry had been reasonable and pushed it one hour to nine thirty, she could've taken Ben herself.

"I'm glad Dad couldn't change the time," Ben said. "This way I get to eat Tori's *delectable* pancakes instead of the oatmeal you make me eat, Mom."

Tori laughed. "Spell *delectable*, mister," she said.

"Too easy." Ben poured more syrup on his pancakes. "Give me something harder."

Allison finished filling her mug with piping-hot fresh brew and stared at Ben in complete awe of him. Only a second-grader, he was the spelling bee champion of his elementary school and would go to nationals next month. He didn't get his brilliance from her, that was for sure.

Although she was Chinese American, she didn't fit any of the East Asian stereotypes and, to her mother's dismay, would never be a member of Mensa. As much as she'd like to take credit for Ben being highly gifted, he got that from his father, along with his thick wavy hair she loved to comb her fingers through, his gentle smile…and penchant for attractive redheads.

A dull ache sliced through her chest. She turned and

grabbed her purse from the counter, not wanting Ben to see a shred of her pain, her anger. Her utter devastation.

"I'll pick you up from school, munchkin," she said, struggling to make her voice sound as carefree as she wanted her son to be. "How about we get gelato?" She faced him and pulled on her best fake smile.

"With Dad?" Ben's chocolate-brown eyes lit up with such hope that it deepened the ache inside her. "Ask him when you see him, please. We haven't done family time in a month."

There was a gelato shop near Balboa Park, where they used to go together, down the street from their favorite Italian place. She and Henry had promised Ben that they'd have a family dinner once a week. But when her soon-to-be ex accepted a position at Quantico and filed for full custody, she'd reneged. Then she'd had to explain it to Ben, without painting his dad as the bad guy. Adding yet another strike against her.

If she got any more, she'd win the award for worst mother of the year. She could set the trophy beside the one for failed marriage on her shelf of shame.

Giving Ben a quick hug, she took in the fruity scent of his shampoo mixed with the sweet aroma of the breakfast Tori had made.

Swallowing past the lump in her throat, she let him go. "I'll ask him."

Provided she didn't strangle Henry during mediation first. No one on the face of the planet made her blood pressure soar or turned her inside out the way he could. The sexy son of a gun could still melt her into pliable putty whenever he touched her and looked at her with that warm gleam in his eyes. No man had ever brought her such pleasure. Or pain.

She was done bending over backward, giving him everything he wanted. D.O.N.E.

Allison headed for the door. "Thanks, Tori, and don't forget to take his new inhaler."

"Got it." Tori waved the small device for Ben's asthma and set it beside him on the counter. "Good luck this morning."

Lord knew Allison needed it. Henry could *not* take Ben. Forget the platitudes about keeping the process civil and reining her emotions. She was going to war.

She left the house and walked to her sedan in the driveway, looking at the uniformed cops sitting in the police cruiser parked in front of her house. They were sipping coffee and chatting while scarfing down fast food from the looks of the paper wrappers littering the dash.

Both were engrossed in their breakfast and conversation when they were supposed to stay sharp, on the lookout. Was this the best protection her boss could get to safeguard her son?

The officers had only been assigned a couple of days ago and had already grown complacent.

Didn't they understand the gravity of the situation?

Dante Emilio Vargas, the leader of *Los Chacales*—the greatest growing threat to national security—not only had it in for the US marshals in San Diego, but he probably had her name on the top of a hit list.

She was the only deputy marshal in her office linked to every single witness who had testified against the cartel and entered WITSEC. Thanks to a breach in their database, that information had fallen into Vargas's hands. He wanted to hurt the US marshals and make them suffer. There was no doubt in her mind that he was gunning for her.

Allison hopped into her Honda Accord, fired up the engine and pulled out. Driving alongside the police cruiser, she rolled her window down and stopped.

"Good morning," she said through their already open window that was letting in the temperate breeze.

"Morning, ma'am," they said in unison.

"I know this isn't the most exciting assignment, but I assure you it's a matter of life or death. I'd appreciate your vigilance."

The two officers nodded with placating grins.

She wanted to rake them over the coals and follow up with a call to their superior, Captain Roessler, ensuring the message had been received. But she stifled a groan and said, "Thanks, guys." *For nothing.*

A whisper of forewarning that something awful was coming, something she was powerless to stop, raised the hairs on the back of her neck.

Allison drove off, praying the FBI finished building their case against Vargas sooner rather than later, threw him behind bars, and put an end to her restless nights fretting that she and her son might be murdered in their sleep.

LOURDES SAT IN the front passenger's seat of the black cargo van. What on earth was she doing there?

There in San Diego instead of a hundred miles away back home in Ensenada, Mexico. There in some quaint suburban part of town, on the corner of a picturesque tree-lined street.

She tapped her petal-pink-painted nails on the car door to keep from chewing them.

"Stop it," her twin brother, Javier, hissed. "I need to focus. I'm working."

That's precisely what worried her. Lourdes was well aware her brother was an assassin for *Los Chacales* cartel. The Jackals.

They called him *El Escorpion*.

He never discussed *business* with her, which she appreciated. She wasn't a fool and understood the house they lived in together had been paid for with blood money. Her lifestyle wasn't extravagant, but it was far better than what she could afford on her meager pay as a teacher, and her brother donated generously to the school to help the students, so she didn't ask questions.

Not until today. "Why am I here, Javier?"

"I need you."

"For what?"

Javier glared at her, warning her to be quiet, and she cringed.

She was closer to him than any other person in the world. For thirty years, they'd been inseparable, yin and yang, speaking every day in person or over the phone when he was away for work, even if it was just a two-minute check-in call. Yet she'd never seen him like this. So intense. So focused. So deadly calm it was frightening.

Then again, she'd never seen him *on the job* before.

A blue Honda rolled past, with a pretty woman behind the wheel, snagging his attention. "That's her."

Before Lourdes could ask the question—*her who?*—Javier raised a gloved hand and pressed a leather-clad finger to his lips.

The silence, the questions tumbling over in her head, the swelling tension in the van, was killing her. He wouldn't even let her turn on the radio or listen to music on her iPhone with earbuds once they'd parked on the corner thirty minutes ago.

He stared at his watch, waiting for something.

It would've been nice to know what the heck that something was.

Five minutes later he said, "It's time." Javier opened a cargo pocket on his black pants, took out a small roll of duct tape, ripped off a strip and placed it over her mouth.

Lourdes shrank back against the door, her eyes growing so wide they felt like they'd pop out of their sockets.

"Lola," he whispered the nickname only he used for her, "you can't scream. I need you to be quiet no matter what. Keep the tape on until I take it off. Nod if you understand."

Her heart was in her throat and her stomach had turned queasy, but she nodded.

Javier put away the tape, started the van and turned right, going in the direction the woman had come from.

Midway down the block, there was a police car parked in front of a two-story Spanish Colonial house. Two cops were laughing hard about something, totally oblivious, as they approached.

Javier rolled down the window and pulled a gun with an attached sound suppressor out of thin air, holding it low in his lap. She hadn't even known he had one handy but had assumed he was packing since he was working.

The street was narrow, no more than thirty feet wide. Javier veered slightly toward the left side of the street. Slowing the van, he aimed and fired twice into the police car through the window, killing both cops. He didn't even stop the vehicle.

A muffled shriek of surprised terror escaped her. If it hadn't been for the tape over her mouth, she would've screamed at the top of her lungs.

Lourdes clung to the door handle, shaking, not quite sure whether she'd bolt from the van. If she did, Javier would only go after her and drag her back to fulfill whatever dark purpose he had in mind. And he'd be angry. Furious.

For all the light and love she projected into the world, her brother radiated something equally powerful. A darkness and a sense of violence that oddly enough drew women to him as much as his money and mesmerizing good looks.

Little did they know he was the scorpion who couldn't help but sting.

But Lourdes knew. He wouldn't want to hurt her, he wouldn't mean to, but his nature had been the same all his life. So she stayed put.

Javier pulled up into the driveway of the Spanish Colonial and parked, but he left the van running.

"Stay here," he ordered. "I'll be back in less than one minute."

She grabbed his arm, looked down at the gun in his right hand and met his eyes. Shaking her head, she silently pleaded with him to stop now and not do whatever he was planning.

"Lola," he said gently, softly, putting his forehead to hers, like when they were little, curled up on a bed, side by side, sharing secrets in the darkness. "I wouldn't have brought you if I didn't need you." He picked up her iPhone and set the timer. "Sixty seconds. No longer. *En mi vida.*" *On my life* in Spanish.

Then he was out of the van. Moving up to the house,

dressed in all black, he was fast and quiet as a wraith, chilling her blood.

He rang the bell, casual as he pleased, as if he were a neighbor or a delivery person.

The front door had a center panel of beveled lead glass. No peephole.

Don't open it. Whoever is inside, don't open the door. Death has come calling.

The front door swung open. Javier raised the gun and swept inside.

Lourdes's heart sank to her toes. *Dear God.* What was he doing?

She looked down at the timer on the phone in her lap. Nanoseconds bled into seconds, an eternity churning in her gut. She glanced at the cop car that had two dead officers inside.

How long would it take her to place a 9-1-1 call?

How many seconds to betray her brother?

She only had thirty left. Not enough time, but even if there was, could she ever turn against him?

To stab him in the back would be the same as plunging a knife into her own heart.

They were more than best friends, more than twins. They'd shared a womb together, yes, but they were joined, connected in a way she couldn't explain. After their parents died when they were eleven, Javier was the one who'd taken care of her. Protected her, fixed her problems, sacrificed and found a way to provide so they never starved or lived on the streets.

Their bond was fierce.

Her joy was his joy. His pain was her pain. There was nothing they wouldn't do for each other. And he needed her.

Not once in all their years together had he ever asked anything of her until now.

It would've been easy to restrain her, to take away her phone, but he hadn't because he trusted her with his own life.

Ten seconds. Nine. Eight.

What to do once it got to one, if he wasn't out of the house?

The front door opened again. A petrified woman with red hair stumbled across the threshold. Her hands were bound behind her back and duct tape covered her mouth.

Javier glided out next, leaving the door open, and carrying…

No, no, no! Lourdes's lungs tightened, squeezing the air from her chest. Shock and fear swamped her. How could he?

He had a child hoisted on his shoulder like a sack of potatoes.

The little boy was gagged, his wrists and ankles bound with zip ties, but he wriggled harder than a worm on a hook determined to get free.

Javier hauled open the side door of the van. He shoved the woman forward with the barrel of his gun. She climbed in, throwing a frantic glance at Lourdes. Javier set the boy down in the van, rolled him farther inside and slammed the door shut.

For several strained heartbeats, Lourdes sat paralyzed and reeling. She couldn't move, couldn't breathe, as she stared at the two hostages.

Javier jumped in behind the wheel and sped backward down the driveway. Cranking the wheel, he

straightened out on the road and threw the van into
Drive.

Zooming down the narrow street, he reached over
and pulled the tape off her lips slowly, showing such
care as if he didn't want to cause her the smallest bit
of pain.

A million questions rushed through her mind, but
she only let one slip through the floodgate of her mouth.
"Why am I here?"

"To keep them calm and quiet." He handed her an
inhaler for asthma. "And to take over for the nanny in
case I have to use her to send a message."

Dread knifed through Lourdes. "What kind of message?"

"A bloody one she won't survive."

Chapter Two

This was going to be a red-letter day that he'd never forget.

Henry shifted in his seat in the conference room, waiting on Ally. Dreading the discussion that would snowball into a full-scale shouting match. He resisted the impulse to loosen his tie. Suits and neckties weren't his style, but his lawyer had insisted.

In the same manner his shark of an attorney had urged him to file for full custody, stressing it was the only way Henry would see Ben for more than summers and Christmas break if he moved to Virginia. All he wanted was an equitable solution, something fair, that took his paternal rights into account and balanced Ally's unreasonable demands.

The timing of when the paperwork had been filed had been god-awful.

He'd hoped to civilly discuss the matter face-to-face with her, after their planned family dinner and once they'd put Ben to bed. But Ally had gotten word about the filing and bailed on pizza and gelato. The very next week, she'd had to go to Los Angeles on a high-priority USMS assignment for ten days.

But they'd talked about it. If one considered her yelling and cursing at him over the phone a discussion.

He wished he'd handled it differently.

Geez, he just kept making the situation worse when he only wanted it to be better, especially for Ben. His son was his main concern now. That's why he'd asked for mediation, cutting out the vicious lawyers who were bleeding them dry, and had the new paperwork in front of him in the manila envelope drawn up.

This needed to end for the sake of everyone's sanity.

He caught sight of Ally marching down the hallway, a take-no-prisoners look stamped on her face. With her smooth complexion and tailored suit showing off her slim, flawless figure, she was lovelier than ever.

It was a lifetime ago when they'd been set up on a blind date by a mutual friend. Henry had thought she resembled the actress Zhang Ziyi, but Ally was more striking. Alluring. Seated across from her at dinner, he had been blown away by how darn beautiful and vivacious she was. Her infectious laugh had immediately lightened his spirt. Her radiance illuminated the world around her.

She'd been an angel, granted more of a warrior archangel, saving him from an empty, lonely life. They'd rushed to the altar after a whirlwind four-week romance, certain they were soul mates, and tried to start a family right away. But it had taken two rounds of IVF for her to get pregnant.

Falling in love had been the only easy part.

Watching her stalk toward the conference room now, he barely recognized the woman he'd once been crazy about.

Who was he kidding?

Even with hellfire blazing in her eyes, he still loved her and always would. But love didn't conquer all.

Ally pushed through the conference room door, head held high, her long black hair pulled into a tight ponytail, her jaw set—ready for battle.

And that was precisely what he wanted to avoid.

She stormed up to the gleaming mahogany conference table. "You can't have him. It doesn't matter how many hours we spend in mediation. That'll never happen."

Why did Allison have to be early?

He rubbed his forehead. Was the mediator going to come back from the bathroom to salvage this before they crossed the point of no return? "Can you sit and listen for a minute?"

"No. You listen. Don't pretend like Ben is suddenly your priority. I carried him for nine months, four of which I spent on bed rest. Alone. Because your job always comes first."

"I didn't have a choice. I was in training."

After her first trimester, he'd been accepted into the thirty-two-week-long Hostage Rescue Team training program. HRT was federal law enforcement's equivalent of Special Forces.

"You could've declined to go," she said. "Requested a different date because of personal circumstances."

"That would've meant waiting a year." To be on the first-tier tactical team had been Henry's dream since he'd joined the FBI. "You didn't run into complications until I'd completed my third week." He shook his head, hating this merry-go-round of blame.

She kept track of every ultrasound and birthday Henry had missed, anniversaries, Ben losing his first tooth, even the cutesy events at preschool, for crying out loud. Not as if she'd been there for all of them, yet only his tally mattered.

"Your mom flew out to help. You weren't alone."

"My mother isn't my husband. You should've been there when he was born," she said, and a deep pang of loss that he hadn't been slashed through him. "Do you know how long I was in labor?"

Forty-one hours.

"Forty-one freaking hours! I almost died in child-birth."

Losing Allison in a divorce was ripping his heart apart, but the prospect of losing her to death was unthinkable. No matter what, she'd always be the only woman for him, his better half in every way.

"Don't you think I wanted to see my kid coming into the world? Cut the umbilical cord? To help you through that?" he asked, his temperature rising as she had the nerve to shrug. "Damn it, Ally. That's not fair."

"I suppose you think it's fair that you decided to accept a position on the other side of the country, without talking to me about it first, and then file for full custody."

"We did discuss it, before…" *The separation.*

"It was a hypothetical conversation before *Sandra* entered the picture."

"She was never in our picture." He gritted his teeth. "I can't advance here in San Diego." The five regional hostage rescue teams had proved successful, but it meant grueling, longer hours, not less, with none of the rewards afforded to those at headquarters. "I can only get promoted by going to Quantico. That was always our plan, and you were supposed to transfer to

Arlington. This is my career we're talking about. Who wants to be stuck in a dead-end job?"

Allison put her hands on her hips. "Once again, it boils down to your career, doesn't it?"

Here we go.

"You're always gone," she said. "For missions. For training. Joint exercises. The past two each had a 120-day cycle. It's a bad, distasteful joke for you to ask for full custody."

Operators were often away from their families for extended periods and called up on a mission with little notice. The time apart was hard on everyone. "We knew when I applied for HRT that sacrifice would be required, and you were on board."

"That was before we had a kid to think of. Before I realized I'd be the only one sacrificing. For you and your career while you had the unmitigated gall to have an affair with—"

"I didn't sleep with her!" Henry wasn't perfect, but he wasn't a cheater. Even though he and Allison hadn't made love in a year, the idea that he'd have sex with someone other than his wife was ludicrous. "How many times do I need to say it? Do you want me to take a lie detector? Because I will. I've got nothing to hide."

"Did they teach you how to beat a lie detector in your elite HRT training?" When he went to answer, she held up her palm. "It doesn't matter. You may not have slept with her, but you crossed the line, Boyd." Ally called him by his last name when she was ticked off at him, and that was a lot lately. "You shared personal information about our marriage with Sandra. About me. By leaning on her, talking to her about your troubles and worries, and letting her comfort you, it was an emotional affair." She threw her hands in the air, huffing a breath. "God, I wish you'd had a one-night stand with her instead."

The words were a sucker punch straight to his gut.

"You don't mean that." Where the hell was the mediator?

"Yes! I do!"

Maybe Allison wasn't attracted to him anymore, if she preferred that he had slept with another woman.

"Well, at least someone would've been touching me." Was that his out-loud voice?

Ally's eyes narrowing to a squint sharp enough to slit his throat told him it had been.

Damn it. You idiot! There was no recovering from that slipup.

"Don't you get the magnitude of the violation?" she asked, refusing to be sidetracked.

It'd been a rough patch in their marriage, a dark time that had continued to fester. Ally wouldn't talk to him, share her pain. Wouldn't let him share his. He didn't recall how he'd started confiding in Sandra, but he'd thought it'd been harmless, helpful, to get a woman's perspective on why Ally had been freezing him out after their loss.

Henry was the best at technical and tactical stuff, and was the first to admit he was sometimes dense as a husband, but Ally had made it painfully clear that on the relationship Richter scale she'd considered the violation a whopping ten.

"I get it," he said.

"What's not fair," she added, rolling full-steam and bulldozing over him, "is that after all that, you still expect me to make more sacrifices for you. My parents are up in San Francisco. They're getting older and soon they're going to need me as much as I'll need them once the divorce is final. I'm not moving to Virginia. You're not taking *my* son with you. And that's final."

There were lots of things he admired about Ally. At the top of the list was her tenacity. It was her superpower, but he never thought the day would come when she'd use it against him.

"You win." He stood, his limbs heavy with defeat, his heart saddled with regret, and held out the paperwork.

Raising a brow, she stared at the manila envelope like it was coated in anthrax. "What's this?"

"Please. Open it."

Ally snatched the envelope from his hand, the look on her face telegraphing that she was prepared to give him no quarter. She took out the papers and, as she read them, the expression drained from her and her forehead creased with confusion.

"You're going to pass on going to Quantico and stay here?" she asked.

He gave a curt nod.

"Uncontested joint custody?" Sheer disbelief rang in her voice as Ally met his resigned gaze, and her battle armor fell to the wayside. "And we alternate weeks that we have him?"

Another nod from him, but the heaviness and guilt only intensified. If he could turn back the clock, he would, but he still wouldn't know how to save his marriage.

She turned to the last page. "You…you signed the divorce papers?" She dropped down into a chair, staring at his signature.

This was more than the death of his professional

aspirations. It was the demise of the only future he'd wanted, with her and Ben, together under one roof as a family.

The divorce had been Ally's idea.

Henry believed in "for better or worse" and had taken his vows seriously. He'd fought for the marriage during their entire separation, which had been one more thing he hadn't desired.

How could they work on their problems, find a way to get closer, reconnect intimately and emotionally by living apart and speaking less? It didn't make any sense to him.

But Ally had kept pushing for space, for time to think. And he'd given it despite the bad feeling in his gut. Then she'd shoved this divorce down his throat.

If this was truly what she needed, he'd let her go and abandon his goal of being assigned at headquarters, so he could be close to Ben. He was done fighting.

"It's everything you initially asked for," he said. "All you have to do is sign and that's it."

"I never thought you'd agree to my terms."

The mediator waltzed into the conference room looking peaked. "Please forgive the delay," she said. "My husband and I are battling food poisoning. We went to the wrong buffet." She sat at the head of the table. "I was going to cancel our session today, but I understand this is an urgent situation for you two."

Henry's cell vibrated in his pocket and Ally's phone rang, as well. He excused himself and took out his mobile while she set the papers down and fished hers from her purse.

He looked at the caller ID. "The office."

Actually, it was his supervisor's direct line. Special

Agent Tobias Keogh was aware Henry was in mediation and wouldn't call unless it was an emergency.

"It's my boss," Ally said, referring to US Marshal Will Draper, who was in charge of the San Diego office.

Every muscle in Henry's body tensed. What were the odds they'd both get a call from work at the exact same time?

He hit the green icon button and put the phone to his ear as Ally answered hers, too. "Boyd here."

"Henry, it's me, Tobias. Brace yourself for what I'm about to say and try to remain calm."

A fist of ice clenched his heart and his gaze flew up to Ally's. She pressed a hand to her stomach, shaking her head in a dazed way as if she had the same sinking sensation.

The mediator's phone pealed with the jarringly distinct sound of an Amber Alert.

Ben?

Oh, God. Please don't let this be about Ben!

Chapter Three

Panic had exploded in Allison, flooding her bloodstream with adrenaline when she'd gotten the news.

Allison, it's Will. Her boss's voice had been taut with strain. *Ben is missing. It looks like he's been taken.*

Her fingers tightened on the steering wheel, knuckles bleaching white, as she raced home.

She clung to the details like a lifeline. The police officers assigned for protection had been murdered. One bullet to each of their heads. A professional hit. Ben was gone! And so was Tori. There were signs of a brief struggle. But no traces of blood in the house.

That meant he was alive. Didn't it?

She held on to desperate hope, rejecting the grim alternative.

Her street was ablaze with red and blue flashing lights. Staring at the yellow crime-scene tape in front of her house, an icy chill skated across her skin.

Neighbors stood on their lawns, gawking at the frenzy of law enforcement. Police. FBI agents. US marshals.

The scene was surreal, almost mind-numbing.

She passed the police car. The bodies had been removed and crime-scene guys surrounded the vehicle, but she glimpsed the fine mist of blood splatter on the headrests. Her gut twisted.

Allison flashed her badge at a uniformed cop blocking her driveway. "This is my house. That's my husband behind me."

The officer nodded and waved her to proceed.

Allison sped a few feet up the driveway and threw her car in Park. She spotted Tobias first. He was a six-foot-three Black guy built like a football player and stood out in a crowd. She knew Tobias well. He and his wife had been to their house regularly for dinner over the years. It was nice being friends with another interracial couple who understood the stresses of societal judgment as well as the pressures of being in federal law enforcement.

Tobias was talking to Will. During her trip to LA, where this situation with Vargas had reached the tipping point, she and her boss had spent a lot of time together and had grown closer as colleagues in the forced proximity with the mutual fear for their families. They were both in Vargas's crosshairs.

Henry parked his SUV to the right of her car. She got out, made her way through personnel, and Henry was right on her heels.

Pushing past Will and Tobias, Ally flew through the open front door and into the house.

A forensics team was crawling over the kitchen, hard at work.

The last thing she wanted to do was contaminate the crime scene, but she needed to see for herself whether there was any blood.

A broken plate was in pieces on the floor, along with a syrup-covered fork next to the stool Ben had been seated in earlier. Less than an hour ago. Stomach acid crawled up her throat.

Another stool had been overturned, but besides that, everything looked in place. Tori's purse and phone were on the counter near the stove. But Ben's inhaler was gone. Hopefully, Tori had managed to grab it in case Ben had an attack.

Her son's backpack was on the hardwood in the exact same spot. No sign of violence.

But Ben had been taken with violence, hadn't he? At gunpoint?

The same weapon that had probably been used to murder two cops had been turned on him and Tori. Blood-chilling images of her son terrified, screaming, being gagged and bound by a professional hit man flashed through her mind.

Was he hurt? Was he crying for her?

She wanted to vomit, but to get through this, for Ben, she needed physical and mental control.

"Honey." Henry's voice or the solid touch of his hand on her shoulder cut through her horrified daze.

The rush of blood roaring in her ears faded. Tearing her gaze from Ben's backpack, she looked at him.

"They need you to leave the kitchen," Henry said quietly, but firmly, and she realized someone from Forensics had spoken to her, but she hadn't heard them.

Nodding, she stepped back. Henry guided her into the living room, where Will, Tobias and police captain Kevin Roessler were waiting for them.

"Mr. and Mrs. Boyd," Captain Roessler said, "we're very sorry about what happened here and we're doing everything we can to locate your son."

"Ally, the first three hours are the most critical."

Tobias directed the statement to her because Henry already knew the statistics, figures and how small a window they had to get Ben back. Reading kidnappers, assessing the volatile, precarious nature of an abduction, the tactics, the firearms, he'd learned by rote. There was no better HRT operator. "Roughly seventy-four percent of kidnap victims who are slain are killed within those first few hours."

Her heart nose-dived to her stomach, but she didn't so much as flinch.

"Most child abductions are custody disputes, but that's not the case here," Tobias said.

She'd been ready to rip out Henry's jugular, thinking he'd be the one to take her son. What she wouldn't give to have Ben safe in Virginia with Henry now, far away from Vargas.

"We'll need a picture of Ben and we're contacting your nanny's family for one of her, as well, to put up on the news," Roessler said, "and for us to use in running a facial recognition scan."

"Her parents are on vacation in Hawaii. They may not have one with them. On the fridge." Allison pointed toward the kitchen. "There's a photo of them together, taken in a booth at a kiddie fun center."

Henry went to go get it.

"We'll also need a description of what they were wearing," Roessler said.

"Ben had on his school uniform. White polo, khakis, sneakers. Tori was wearing, um, jeans and a flowy powder-blue top that had little red flowers all over it."

Henry came back into the room and handed Roessler the photo.

"We have to work quickly," Tobias said. "Our best

chance of following any leads is within the first forty-eight hours. Once we hit seventy-two—"

"Do you have any leads?" Henry asked, cutting him off.

They only had seventy-two hours. No, make that seventy-one.

They had to find him before then. She didn't want to consider the ugly possibilities after that. But what would she do if she lost him?

A wave of dizziness engulfed her. Swaying for a second, she struggled to stay on her feet, but did. Her reaction was staggering. She was a hard-nosed marshal, who kept a level head, made tough judgment calls even at her own personal risk, but right now she felt like jelly.

Helplessness and fear gripped her chest, tightened her throat, making it ache. But she took all those overwhelming emotions and redirected them, letting it fuel her rage.

Fury she'd wield like a weapon and use to find her son. Anything to stave off thinking, to sublimate feeling despair.

"A neighbor walking his dog spotted a black van racing away from your house," Captain Roessler said, "found my murdered officers and called 9-1-1. But he didn't see the driver and only got a partial license plate number. We're combing through CCTV footage within a ten-block radius of your home to get a hit on the vehicle."

"Why is everyone standing around ignoring the damn elephant in the room?" Allison asked. "We know who took Ben. It was Vargas. Get a warrant and get my son."

As Roessler and Tobias looked away from her, Will

said, "Our hands are tied. We can't get a warrant based on our assumptions. We need evidence to get a judge to sign off."

"What if it was Noah?" she asked, referring to Will's teenage son. "Or Sylvia and Monica?" she asked Tobias about his girls. "What if Vargas had sent someone to your home and snatched your children? Untie some hands. Call in a favor. Between a police captain, the special agent in charge and a US marshal for San Diego, you should be able to do something. I'm not asking you to part the Red Sea. I'm begging you to help me get my little boy back."

Will took a deep breath. "We've both dreaded this. I know how you feel."

"No. You don't." He couldn't possibly. Imagining your worst fear and living the actual nightmare were nothing alike.

"We're doing everything we can," Roessler said.

"Well, it's not enough," she snapped. "It's your fault this happened. Those two cops you assigned were complacent. More concerned about their breakfast than keeping my kid safe."

"Whoa, lady. You're talking about two good officers who are dead." Roessler put his fists on his hips and stepped forward, getting in her face, but Henry swept in front of him as a buffer, easing him back. "Now their widows have to plan funerals and their kids will never see their fathers again. From what I've heard this morning, you marshals are the ones who messed up. Wasn't one of your own responsible for some data breach?"

Henry threw her a quick, perplexed glance and shifted his gaze to Roessler. "Please give our condolences to the families of those officers," Henry said.

"We know you all are doing everything in your power to help us."

Allison thought about those cops blowing her off this morning, saw their mocking grins. "I'm not sorry. I meant what I said."

"Excuse us." Henry took her by the elbow, hauled her down the hall into the laundry room and slammed the door closed.

"Don't ever answer for me," she said. "What makes you think you can speak for me?"

"Those cops were killed protecting our son. What are you thinking? Have you lost your mind trashing them to their captain?"

"What I said about them was true. If they'd been vigilant, Ben might still be with us." She was sorry they'd been killed, leaving behind families, but her pain was a living, breathing monster inside her that she wanted to unleash on the world.

"It doesn't change the fact that we need the help of the SDPD. And what did Roessler mean about how the marshals messed up? You came back from your assignment in LA and told me that because of the heat you guys put on Vargas, Draper thought it was a good idea to assign everyone in your office protection. What data breach?"

"Why did you insist on the mediation appointment first thing this morning?" Hot tears stung the backs of her eyes. "Why couldn't you pick a later time after I dropped him off at school, where he would've been safe?"

"Don't you dare deflect. Don't try to spin this around. What aren't you telling me?"

She stood still as stone, but inside her guts started

quivering. Her very soul shuddered at what Vargas might do to her helpless baby.

Deep down, she wasn't pointing the finger of responsibility at Roessler or the dead officers, or Henry.

She was the one to blame. Wasn't her *one* job above everything else to keep Ben safe?

"It's my fault," she whispered.

Henry clasped her shoulders, drawing closer. "What are you talking about?"

"I should've told you." But she'd stopped sharing in so many little ways that had only grown bigger, swelling until they filled the space between them like a hundred balloons she didn't know how to pop. "Do you remember the yearlong assignment to protect a witness up at Big Bear Lake?"

"Yeah, of course. I'd been so upset that you had even contemplated taking it when it meant a year away from us."

She'd only considered it to show him what it felt like to be the one left behind, holding down the proverbial fort while being a single parent. Countless opportunities she'd missed while he'd got to live his dream.

"The witness, Lori Carpenter—the one I got settled up in Big Bear before handing her off to two others—her testimony crippled the main money-laundering engine for Vargas and his cartel. To make matters worse, Vargas had been involved with her."

Henry's brow creased with worry lines. "So, it was personal for him as well as financial?"

She nodded. "Vargas had turned one of the marshals assigned to protect her and he handed over a classified laptop."

"What?"

"Vargas hacked our system. Full breach. The names of every witness that has been relocated here in California. As well as the personal information of every marshal in this state."

Henry's curse was low and foul. He let her go and ran a hand through his dark, wavy hair.

"There's more." She had to keep going, spew out the rest before she lost her nerve. "Vargas had planned to auction the data off to the highest criminal bidder. My assignment up in LA was to support another marshal in recruiting an asset. Vargas's niece. Isabel helped us wipe the hard drive that he had, ensuring the big auction never happened. Vargas was extremely close to her. I'm sure he didn't take the betrayal well."

She took a shaky breath. "My office has done nothing but cause Vargas endless trouble. Will stands out because he's in charge, but my name is connected to every witness that's testified against Vargas. Will didn't authorize protection for everyone in my office. The SDPD manpower requirement was too high. He only got approval for our two families because he knew we'd be the most likely targets if Vargas sought retribution."

A muscle popped in Henry's jaw. His eyes were hard, his lips pressed tight. Deep furrows marked his brow. "You didn't think I had a right to know that?"

Guilt stabbed her between the ribs. If they'd still been in the same house, sharing a bed, she would've spilled her guts about the debacle in her office.

But she hadn't been able to let go of her anger that'd started to taint everything between them. A blight spreading in the darkness that he'd fed and encouraged the second he'd filed for full custody.

"You tried to take Ben away. Something I never

thought you'd do. My lawyer told me the only time a father doesn't go along with joint custody of a small child is when there's something seriously wrong with the mother. He was convinced you were going to play hardball and warned me not to give you any ammunition. If you knew Vargas might come after me..." She shook her head, sickened to her core.

If anything happened to Ben, it was her fault for being selfish, for being scared.

"Damn lawyers," Henry said. "I never should've listened to mine and filed those papers to begin with. It was only a tactic to get you to negotiate. To be reasonable. I'd never take him from you. Still, it was wrong of me, but that doesn't excuse what you did. Lying to me. Hiding the fact that you and Draper were targets. How could you?" He looked like he might spit nails at her.

She braced for him to really launch into her, tell her what she already realized. How stupid she'd been. If only she'd had the strength to set aside her anger and pride and told him. Why had she believed Henry would've used it against her to bolster his claim for full custody?

The man she fell in love with and married would've taken time off and moved back in until the situation with Vargas was resolved. One of them could've been with Ben every second that he wasn't in school. The mediation appointment never would have happened.

She'd left Ben vulnerable. Exposed.

"Say it." She trembled, quaking down to her bones with self-loathing and fear for how her son might pay for her mistakes. "Go on. I deserve to hear it."

Henry banded his strong arms around her, pulling her into a hug. The familiar scent of his aftershave enveloped her. She sank against the muscular shelter of his body, the embrace that was always so safe, felt so much like home.

Though he wasn't her haven anymore, she soaked in the comfort he offered, only enough to take the edge off.

"I've got you, angel." His soothing voice sent a rush of warmth through Allison, chasing away the chill beneath her skin. "I'm sorry I made you feel like you couldn't talk to me. Couldn't trust me with the truth."

His sincerity, his tenderness, was unmistakable and completely unexpected. She swallowed hard, uncertain how to respond. It was too much and something inside her threatened to snap, but she couldn't let the bottled-up anguish surface. Then she'd lose control.

She drew back and stared up into Henry's face. His features were etched by sadness and pain, but also love.

"I'm here for you and for our son. Always will be." Henry gripped her shoulders tight. "When we leave this room, we are united. One team, one fight. Okay?"

She nodded, too emotional to speak.

"We're going to get our boy back. Whatever it takes. I swear it."

Chapter Four

They drove through Barrio Logan—a predominantly Mexican suburb Lourdes had been to once before while on vacation with her brother. Javier turned into a gas station, avoiding the pumps, and went around the back to the detached garage housing an automated car wash.

Her mind whirled with worry and too many questions lacking answers. They had just kidnapped a child and his nanny. Why was her brother taking the time to wash the stupid van?

At the unmanned payment station, he selected the options he wanted on the machine and turned to her. "This is a good time to check on them. You can remove their gags as long as they agree to behave. If either of them is foolish enough to scream, no one will hear them while we're in there." He gestured to the car wash.

Pulling up to the opening, he started aligning the wheels with the track system.

Lourdes stuffed the inhaler into the pocket of her jeans and shoved past the seats into the rear of the van. She knelt in front of the boy, who was on his side, and sat him up next to the nanny. Brushing his dark hair from his eyes, she stroked his forehead softly and caressed his cheek, taking in his tearstained face.

He was a cute boy, maybe eight years old. Right around the same age as her kids.

Lourdes wasn't a mother and never would be. When she was seventeen, she'd gotten pregnant by her no-good boyfriend. She'd been too young to have a baby on her own and decided to end the pregnancy, thinking one day she'd get married and have a house full of little ones.

But the "doctor" she'd gone to hadn't known what he was doing. Javier had made sure that man never messed up another woman's body.

Thinking back on it, she wondered if the doctor was the first person her brother had ever killed. Had Javier become a murderer because of her? Or had there been someone else before that?

The ordeal had given her pause with men, made her fearful of sex, but it had also led to her teaching. Every year, the thirty kids in her class were hers, to shape and guide and care for. And Javier helped out however he could, buying supplies and treats for all the students at her school. The lives of so many children had been enriched and made better because of him.

The wash track system engaged, jerking the van and pulling it forward into the garage, and the interior space grew dark. The boy's watery brown eyes widened, his gaze darting around frantically as the vehicle shook under the sudden pressure of the water jets.

"It's okay, nothing to be afraid of," she said to him in the voice she used whenever she needed to calm her students. Soft but authoritative. "We're in a car wash. You've been inside one before, right?"

The boy nodded. His breathing started to slow down.

"Do you both promise not to scream if I take off the tape?" she asked him and the nanny.

They nodded.

Gently, Lourdes peeled off the boy's gag. "Are you all right? Are you hurt?"

"I'm fine," he whispered.

Sudsy foam covered the windshield in thick white lather.

"Good," she said, removing the tape from the nanny's mouth. "What are your names?"

"Benjamin, but everyone calls me Ben."

"Tori."

The large brushes of the car wash moved back and forth over the van.

"I'm Lourdes. How old are you, Ben?"

"Seven. Almost eight."

"You're a big boy for your age." Lourdes sat back on her heels. Resting her hands on her hips, she felt the inhaler in her pocket. "Ben, do you have asthma?"

"Yes," he said, nodding. "But I left my inhaler at the house."

"My brother grabbed it for you. Don't worry." Lourdes gave a sheepish smile, doing her best to act like the situation was normal.

The redheaded woman glanced at Javier and then looked back at Lourdes. "You have to help us," she said too low for Javier to hear over the pounding water jets. "Please, cut us loose. Open the doors and we'll run."

Ben whimpered, his eyes filling with tears. "I want my mommy." He turned, burying his face in the nanny's shoulder.

Lourdes's heart squeezed at the sight of him crying and shaking. "Shh. You're upsetting him." She put the tape back over Tori's mouth. "I am here to help you, but not to escape. I can't do that. I'm sorry." She stroked Ben's head over and over until he settled a bit. "I want us to be friends." She cupped his chin, encouraging him to look at her, and wiped at his tears. "I'll do everything I can to keep you safe, but you have to listen to me and my brother. Do whatever we ask. All right?"

Ben sniffled, still softly crying. "Okay."

The van eased forward into the sunlight.

Lourdes got up and went back to the passenger's seat. To her astonishment, the hood of the van was now a gleaming white.

The black paint had been temporary and came clean off in the car wash.

Did her brother do this sort of thing all the time?

He was a professional. A terrifying, skilled assassin, and apparently a kidnapper.

Javier drove three blocks to Chicano Park. The first time she'd seen it, Lourdes had fallen in love with that park—home to one of the largest outdoor murals in the United States, dedicated to the cultural heritage of the local community.

He stopped the van under the San Diego–Coronado Bridge. "I've got to change the license plate in case anyone saw it earlier." He grabbed a new plate from under his seat, along with a screwdriver, and hopped out.

"Lourdes," Ben called.

She got up, shuffled to the back and knelt beside him. "What's up, little buddy?"

"I have to pee."

"Do you think you can hold it?"

He scrunched his face like he might have an accident in the van. "I had a lot of milk with my pancakes.

I really have to go. Right now." He pulled his knees up to his chest and rocked.

"Okay," she said, not wanting the poor boy to soil himself.

She grabbed a pair of scissors Javier had stashed in the glovebox, cut the zip ties on Ben's ankles and wrists, and slipped the shears in her back pocket.

Helping him to his feet, she ushered him to the side door and slid it open.

Javier came from the rear of the van. "What's going on?" he asked, looking around.

She hadn't thought to check their surroundings first, but no one was nearby. "He's got to tinkle. He can't hold it." She closed the van door.

"Let him go by that pillar and keep an eye on him. The kid has one minute."

Lourdes now knew when her brother said *one minute* that was precisely what he meant.

Holding Ben by the shoulders, she hustled him to the stone pillar her brother had indicated. "Hurry up. My brother isn't a patient man."

"I can't go with you watching. My mommy said peeing is private."

Lourdes sighed and turned around. "Better?"

"No. I'm too nervous," he said with a brittle voice. "Can you sing to me?"

Sing?

Her gaze flickered to the colorful murals in the area as she racked her brain for a song. The first one to pop into her mind with some English lyrics she could recall was "Rain Over Me" by Marc Anthony and Pitbull.

Bopping to the beat she heard in her head, she sang a couple of verses low. "'Ay ay ay, ay ay ay, let it rain over me.'" She repeated the lyrics and as she segued into Pitbull's rap, she glanced over her shoulder.

But the boy was gone.

Panic seared through her. Ben had bolted and was in a full-on sprint at least twenty yards away.

Oh, no.

"Javier!" Lourdes took off after him, not waiting for a response from her brother.

She darted down the street as fast as her sneakers would carry her. But Ben was quicker. The little boy ran like the devil.

He reached a street corner and stopped. Looking up at the lamppost, he waved his hands back and forth in front of it as if signaling, but there was no one around.

What is he doing? Why didn't he keep running?

Javier blasted past her, his long legs eating up the distance. His boots pounded the asphalt with every step as he stormed toward the kid.

Ben's panic-stricken eyes locked on her brother and the boy dashed around the corner.

Javier charged down the street at a startling pace. He was in the finest physical condition, his body honed with dedication, but the ferocious strides he took left her breathless.

The boy and her brother disappeared out of sight around the corner.

Her heart was a jackhammer in her chest. Her lungs were on fire. Pumping her arms harder, she tore around the corner and ran down the street toward the grassy field.

There was a group of women gathered around a park table. A bunch of kids too young to be in elementary school were running around on the playground a few feet away.

Ben launched into the cluster of mothers and pointed at Javier, who was almost on them.

Panting, Lourdes pushed harder. She didn't worry about getting air into her lungs, only focused on exhaling and driving her legs faster before there was a bloodbath.

The women circled around Ben like a pack of lionesses prepared to protect a lost cub.

Javier slowed and approached the women, drawing within arm's reach, and was saying something to them.

Sweet Lord! Help me!

Ben clutched his chest and dropped. One of the mothers caught him and the others formed a blockade, not letting Javier any closer.

Lourdes gave it everything she had, but by the time she reached them, she was too winded to speak. Her stomach convulsed as if she might vomit. Putting her hands on her knees, she bent over and raked in air.

"I'm with *Los Chacales*," Javier said. "Do you know what that means?"

The six women exchanged terrified glances that said they knew exactly what it meant.

"That boy is my property," Javier said. "You don't want to come between me and what's mine. Give him to me."

The woman holding Ben put his head to her chest, tightening her other arm around him. "Someone call 9-1-1."

Ben was wheezing badly, as though his airways strained for oxygen, and his eyes closed.

A different mother grabbed her cell phone.

Javier whipped out his gun from under his shirt and pointed it at the women. "If you try to take that kid, I'll kill one of you."

The woman with the phone in her hand gasped. She dropped the cell and raised her palms.

Lourdes stepped beside Javier. "You don't have to do this."

"Shut up!" he said to her, then turned back to the women. "Is the life of that boy worth one of yours? Decide now who is going to let their child watch them die." He released the safety and cocked the gun.

The laughter of children filled the air. Lourdes's heart twisted inside her chest and dread clogged her throat.

The woman holding Ben laid him on the grass and all the mothers backed away from him. Regret and shame hung on their faces.

But what choice did they have?

"Lola." Javier looked at her. "He needs the medicine."

The command cleared her head and spurred her into action. Taking the inhaler from her pocket, Lourdes ran to Ben. She dropped to her knees, shook the device, put it in his mouth and pumped it twice.

"Give me your phones," Javier said to the women.

Without hesitation, they handed over their mobile devices. He removed the batteries, tossed them and smashed the screens under his boot heel.

The high-pitched whistling sound coming from Ben eased. His eyes fluttered open. It took him a minute to focus on her face. The kid looked drained, totally wiped out, and his skin was pale.

Javier put away his gun, stowing it in the back of

his waistband, and came up next to her. He knelt and scooped Ben up in his arms. Without saying a word to her, he stood and took off, headed back to the van.

"I'm sorry," Lourdes said to the frightened women before jogging after her brother.

The distance to the van somehow seemed shorter. She got there as Javier opened the door and set Ben gently inside and restrained his hands and ankles again with zip ties.

Her brother grabbed Tori by the hair. She winced in pain, unable to cry out with tape covering her mouth or fight back since she was still restrained.

"What are you doing?" Lourdes said.

Javier shoved her backward with one hand so hard that Lourdes stumbled and hit the ground. Gravel bit into her palms.

"This is on you!" he snapped at her.

His eyes were full of rage and she had to remind herself that not only did she love him, she also owed him everything. Without him, she probably would've been dead in a ditch at twelve, or worse.

Turning, he glared at Ben, his grip still firm on Tori's hair. "Do you want me to hurt her?"

"No." Ben's voice was weak and hoarse. "Please, don't."

"If you run again, your nanny pays the price. I'll put a bullet in both of her knees. Do you understand?"

Tears leaked from Ben's eyes. "Yes."

Javier released Tori, letting her face hit the van floor, and slammed the door closed. Spinning on his heel, he wrenched Lourdes up from the ground by her arm.

"The boy is too smart for his own good. That streetlight," he said, pointing to the lamppost where Ben had stopped and waved his arms, "is one of the new ones with cameras. CCTV. The authorities will know we were here. They'll have my face and yours. The one good thing is they'll be looking for a black van. We weren't supposed to cross the border, but now we have no choice. My employer won't be happy."

The head of *Los Chacales*. Fear welled in her chest. Would something bad happen to Javier because she'd messed up? Had she endangered his life?

"Tell him it was my fault," Lourdes said, her voice heavy with apology. "It was my mistake. If someone has to be punished, it should be me."

Javier grabbed her face in his hands, startling her. He stared into her eyes with an intensity that sent a chill through her, but he brought her forehead to his. "If there are repercussions, I'll handle it." His voice was strained but soft. "I'll never let anything happen to you, Lola. Never."

Not wanting him to see the tears blurring her vision, she squeezed her eyes shut. "I'm sorry." Guilt ran through her. "I wasn't thinking." She'd been so stupid.

"The boy is clever. Don't underestimate him. And no matter what, never turn your back on him again."

Chapter Five

The brand-new burner phone buzzed against his chest. After the failed auction, Emilio Vargas had replaced all his mobile devices and had his home swept for bugs. Necessary precautions that were the tip of the iceberg.

He retrieved the cell from his inner suit jacket pocket. *"Dígame,"* he said into the phone. *Tell me.*

"I have the boy."

"Very good." Smiling, Emilio strolled from his villa outside into the sunshine. "Give me a minute." He passed Lucas, one of his guards, and walked out of the man's earshot, taking a seat in the manicured courtyard that overlooked the ocean. A pleasant breeze carried the heady scent of mock orange blossoms. "Is he unharmed?"

"Yes," Javier, *El Escorpion*, said. "But there's been a complication. The kid made a run for it. He was caught on CCTV. So was I."

Emilio muttered a curse under his breath, the sweet taste of triumph turning bitter in his mouth. "It's not like you to make such a mistake. Why didn't you sedate him?"

"You told me he had a medical condition. I didn't want to risk it."

Javier was the right ruthless killer for the job. He was the best in his profession, careful and shrewd.

The last thing Emilio wanted was for the kid to die accidentally. He needed the child alive to get what he wanted. If the marshal didn't cooperate, well, then no guarantee the boy would keep breathing. His life was in Emilio's hands. If it came to a premature end, then it must be a deliberate, well-considered move—checkmate.

"I don't think it's a good idea to take him to Chula Vista," Javier said.

A place had already been prepared there in the suburb of San Diego. Isolated, with no nosy neighbors around, stocked with food and games for the child.

"Are you sure you can't make it work?" Emilio asked.

"I strongly advise against it. This city is the fifth most surveilled in the country. There are ten thousand new surveillance sensors on streetlights alone. They'd find us before you were able to fully execute your plan."

Emilio gritted his teeth. Nothing could stand in the way of this. *Absolutely nothing.* "I can't allow that."

Those infuriating marshals had been working overtime to destroy his empire. Coercing those in his inner circle to betray him. They had gotten to his lover, Lori, and had used her to crush his main money-laundering conduit. That had galled him to the bone. But then they'd dared infiltrate his home and put a stop to the auction he'd promised important colleagues. They'd humiliated him in front of the crème de la crème of the crime syndicates.

Even more grievous, they'd manipulated his beloved Isabel, turning her against him, and whisked her away to only God knew where.

They had finally gone too far. Crossed an unforgivable line. Emilio would see to it those bastards paid, and he would show no mercy.

"What do you propose?" he asked.

"Let me take him and the nanny to Ensenada. I can keep them contained there. I'm already at the border. I just need your blessing to cross."

"What if I need to send the mother a message, showing her I'm *deadly* serious?" Emilio had something special in mind for Allison Chen-Boyd, the one marshal tied to every single traitor. Not only did he seek to instill fear and remorse in her heart, he would make an example out of her, dragging her to depths she'd never imagined. Taking her peace of mind was just the beginning. "Can you make it happen in a reasonable amount of time from that location?"

"Of course."

"All right. Notify me at once if there are further complications."

"There won't be." Javier's voice was steady and lethally sure.

That was the response Emilio wanted to hear. "In the event of a worst-case scenario, I need you to do two things for me."

"I'm listening."

Emilio relayed his instructions in explicit detail. "Only as a last resort," he added, hoping such severe action wouldn't be required. If Isabel ever found out, he'd lose her forever.

"Very well. I'll see to it both things are done if there's no other recourse."

Emilio put away the burner phone as Rodrigo, his top lieutenant, came outside along with Max, one of his enforcers.

"We found out the Amber Alert that came through was for the US marshal's kid," Rodrigo said. "The one woman you hate the most. Was it us? Did we take him?"

These days Emilio had to compartmentalize everything for operational security. Not to mention personal safety.

The marshals had gotten closer and closer each time. His lover. And then…*Isabel.* His precious daughter he hadn't been permitted to raise as his own, forced to let her believe she was his niece. Until the marshals had meddled in his affairs and ruined everything.

One good thing had come from the debacle with the auction. The head of the Yakuza on the west coast had learned Emilio had yet another traitor in his midst. The FBI had either planted a mole within his ranks or turned one of his men as an informant. Someone who knew how Emilio's organization worked. Someone he trusted.

No longer could he afford to trust anyone with everything.

Unless there was an excellent need to know, it was none of Rodrigo's or Max's damn business if he'd abducted the child.

"Very interesting," Emilio said. "Perhaps karma is taking care of her for me."

"It wasn't us?" Max asked, scratching his goatee.

"If I took the child, don't you think I would've told you about my plans?"

Max and Rodrigo exchanged a glance that was hidden behind their sunglasses.

"Of course you would've, Don Emilio," Rodrigo said, straightening his spine. "It's just you've been acting different lately."

Because I have a snake in my house.

But I shall bait the reptile, catch it and chop off its head.

"We can't protect you if we don't know what's going on," Max said.

Emilio crossed his legs and steepled his fingers. "Keep me abreast of the situation. If you hear anything else about the missing child, be sure to let me know."

"Things have been *quiet* for us the past few days," Rodrigo said, referring to the sudden hiatus the men thought they were on. "Is there anything we can do for you? To ease what happened with Isabel?"

Emilio's heart ached in a way that it hadn't in decades. Not since Isabel's mother had died from cancer. He breathed through it, summoning his rage. The US marshals would know firsthand his pain. Experience his suffering. "Come to think of it, there is something you can do. Lucas!" Emilio called, beckoning to his bodyguard.

Once Lucas had joined Rodrigo and Max, Emilio looked between them. One of the men standing before him was a traitor working for the FBI.

"I want you to get me C-4," Emilio said.

"How much?" Rodrigo asked.

"Twenty bricks."

His men shared a look with one another.

A tiny amount of the high-yield chemical explosive packed a punch. Each brick weighed more than a pound.

Twenty-five pounds would demolish half a city block, and Emilio planned to use every ounce.

Lucas and Max clasped their hands behind their backs and buttoned their lips.

"May we know what it's for?" Rodrigo asked, as any lieutenant worth his salt would.

Emilio smiled. "In due course." But without haste and only once they had a need to know.

ALLISON PACED IN the living room, wringing her hands.

Forensics had cleared out, but the house was abuzz with the FBI setting up in the dining room alongside detectives to monitor their calls and emails for when Ben's *kidnapper* contacted them. Technically, this was the jurisdiction of local law enforcement since there was no evidence of interstate transportation.

But the FBI took an interest in all abductions involving a missing child of *tender years*, twelve and younger. And this case concerned one of their own.

"You should sit," Henry said, loosening his tie and taking it off. "It might take some time before we hear anything." He undid the top button of his dress shirt.

Time was exactly what they didn't have. How could he expect her to sit when a monster had taken her baby?

Henry's grace under fire was one of his best qualities. She needed his strength, to draw on the calm he exuded, but asking her to do nothing was pointless.

"He's been missing three hours," she said. "We have to do more than wait around. I can't stand this helplessness."

Tobias poked his head around the corner from the dining room. "Hey, guys. We've got something you should probably see."

Allison and Henry hurried into the next room.

Tobias gestured for them to come around the table and positioned them in front of a laptop. "SDPD have been scanning CCTV for the black van and Henry. Facial recognition got a hit." Tobias tapped the enter button and a video played. "This was recorded about an hour and a half ago."

The screen was split into four different views of one location. New streetlights had been fitted with several sensors, including multiple cameras and audio that would detect gunshots or the sound of breaking glass.

In the background of one angle was a brick building and a taller structure. "Is that the Coronado Bridge?" she asked.

"Yes." Tobias nodded.

A little boy came onto the screen. *Ben!* Allison gasped, putting a hand over her mouth. He ran up to the streetlight and waved in front of the camera.

He got away. Her son got away from his captor.

"Good boy," Henry whispered.

Ben glanced back over his shoulder and took off with a frightened look. The abject fear splashed across her child's face made her blood run cold.

If only there was something that she could do to help him.

Seconds later, a man tore after him like a bullet.

Her baby would never be able to outrun him. The guy was lean, but looked sinewy, hardened, and was way too fast. Her chest squeezed so hard she could barely breathe.

That was who'd taken their son for Vargas. It had to be.

From another camera, she watched Ben and the man enter the field of a park, but that was all she could see. She pressed a hand to her forehead, trying to pinpoint exactly where they were.

Chicano Park. Only fifteen minutes from the house.

A woman ran in the same direction. Her long, dark

hair flowed behind her as she chased after them. She appeared to be in her late twenties, maybe early thirties, like the man who was stalking her son.

The three of them had disappeared from the screen.

Oh, God. What was happening? Any minute Ben's asthma would kick in. Where was Tori? Did she have his inhaler?

Henry put an arm around Allison's shoulder. She clenched a hand in a fist and bit down on her index finger, her muscles drawing tight.

Maybe Ben was able to hide. He could've ducked behind something and given them the slip.

But deep down, she knew that wasn't true.

The man appeared again, running, but at a slower pace. This time he was carrying Ben. Her son lay limp in his arms, not struggling.

Was he all right? Had he had an asthma attack? Had the man hurt him, trying to stop him? Why wasn't Ben resisting?

The woman raced up behind them. As they drew nearer the bridge, they left the range of the camera and were no longer within view.

"What happened to him?" she asked. "Is Ben okay?"

"We're not sure, but we think so," Tobias said. "Officers have been dispatched to the park to canvass the area and see if anyone saw anything."

"This is a decent lead," Henry said in an encouraging voice, but she sensed his worry in the way he squeezed her shoulder.

Tobias tapped on the keyboard and brought up four snapshots. Two were close-ups of the woman and man who had her son.

"We're going to get their pictures out there. The entire city will be on the lookout for them."

"What's that?" Henry asked, dropping his arm from around her and pointing to the third picture, which captured the back of the man's hand as he carried Ben.

"It's a tattoo. We think that man is *El Escorpion*. A known hit man for *Los Chacales*."

Allison sucked in a breath as her stomach bottomed out.

"Are you sure?" Henry asked.

"We can't be certain because no one has ever seen him. He's only ever been identified by the tattoo of the scorpion on his right hand."

Henry's jaw tightened. "He sent a hit man to snatch our kid?"

Allison stared at him. "Why would Vargas do that unless he planned to kill him?"

"Don't think like that," Tobias said. "Maybe he wanted a professional who could easily eliminate the police detail and it doesn't mean anything more. If he wanted your boy dead, *El Escorpion* would've done it here in the house. Or shot Ben when he ran."

Everything Tobias said was terrifyingly true and did little to alleviate her concern.

"The last picture?" Henry pointed at the screen.

Tobias enlarged it. The woman had Ben's inhaler in her hand.

Thank God. They had his medicine.

"They chased him instead of shooting him, and they have his inhaler," Tobias said. "Solid indicators that they want your son to remain alive and well."

"Tori?" she asked. "Was there any sign of her?"

Tobias shook his head. "She may have been in the

van or subdued somewhere in the vicinity. The police searched CCTV of the area for the black van in question, hoping to track it, but none turned up."

Henry crossed his arms. "They might've changed vehicles."

"It's possible. But if they did, it'll make it that much harder to find them." Tobias sighed. "Let's focus on the positives. We have confirmation that Ben is alive. He's a smart kid and can think in a crisis when some adults freeze or unravel."

Allison turned to Henry. "How did he know about the cameras and to wave?"

"We watched an action-adventure cartoon about a female modern-day Robin Hood and CCTV was mentioned in one episode. I pointed out what some of the cameras really looked like around town and explained how it all works."

She put her palm to his chest, grateful Henry had taught Ben things that had never occurred to her. He covered her hand with his. She held his gaze, unable to look away, her heart swelling.

How had they gotten to this place, grown so far apart?

The miscarriage had triggered an avalanche in their marriage. Things had kept mounting, one offense after another, until they'd finally been buried beneath a mound of hurt too deep to escape.

No matter their issues as husband and wife, or her complaints about the demands of his job, there was no question he was a great father.

"I'll put on a pot of coffee," Tobias said, and they pulled apart.

"How is this supposed to work?" she asked Henry. "What's the next step?"

"We wait for ransom demands." He guided Allison back into the living room and to the sofa, taking a seat beside her.

"I can't stand this." She cradled her head in her hands.

"I'm not used to it, either, being on the other side of things. But we don't have a choice. We don't know where Ben is, and we don't know what Vargas wants."

There was always a choice.

Henry propped his elbows on his thighs and clasped a palm over his fist. "We can't even be certain it was Vargas who took him. Maybe it was someone else with a grudge and a different agenda."

Marshals and FBI agents didn't advertise their identities. Before today, their neighbors only knew they were in federal law enforcement.

No one held a grudge against Henry, besides her, and he'd given her just cause.

Other than Vargas and Sandra, Allison didn't have any enemies.

People liked her. She operated well in a team at work and she was that person neighbors borrowed eggs or a cup of sugar from. A member of the PTA, even though she didn't make all the meetings, parents counted on her to bring an extra tray of brownies to the bake sales for someone who'd forgotten.

Her profession had never been a danger to her son until the data breach.

There wasn't a doubt in her mind who'd taken Ben. Thanks to their system being compromised, Vargas knew the names of the US marshals responsible for hurting his cartel. He had every reason in the world to hate the marshals and the means to wreak havoc on their lives.

"Even Tobias thinks *El Escorpion* was the man caught on CCTV," she said. "A known associate of *Los Chacales*."

"It's conjecture, not confirmation." As he bowed his head, Henry's shoulders slumped. "Those types of hit men might have a main employer, but they're known to do freelance work. I'd like certainty. To get demands that we can work with. Start negotiating to get him back." He let out a heavy breath and his warm brown eyes found hers. "It could take a while. Do you mind if I camp out at the house if it comes to that?"

He still had some clothes there and basic toiletries in the cabinet under their bathroom sink. But the third bedroom, which had been the nursery, he'd turned into a gym after they lost the baby, and she couldn't expect him to sleep on the sofa with a house full of people.

"It only makes sense," she said. "You need to be here."

"I can bunk in his room." His throat worked spastically as he swallowed. "Until we get him back."

On the twin bed? Surrounded by all of Ben's things?

God, she wouldn't put him through that.

"There's plenty of space for you in our room." Allison put a hand on Henry's leg. His muscles tensed beneath her palm and a ripple of awareness ran through her veins.

Henry was one of those rare men who got better looking with age, cuter, sexier. So utterly unfair.

It was hard to believe they hadn't shared a bed for six months. Even longer since they'd made love, but it had felt like forever. They'd once been so close, so passionate and hungry for each other.

Her mind flashed on that night at the bar. Henry had begged her to meet him for drinks with his coworkers. When she'd showed up and overheard part of his conversation with Sandra, she'd lost it. Had seen red and gone ballistic that he'd shared intimate things about their marriage and their problems with another person, much less an attractive woman who spent more time with him at the office than Allison did at home.

Henry hadn't gotten defensive or angry in return. He'd just stared at her, looking lost. Like she'd spoken a foreign language. Once again it was as if they were on two separate pages in different books.

She dropped her hand and shifted on the cushions. "I don't think we should sit here and wait." That was what Vargas expected, what he wanted. "I have a better idea."

Chapter Six

His heart was in turmoil as Ally dropped her gaze and withdrew from him, physically and emotionally, and the grim reality of it hurt.

He wanted to reel her closer, to fix things. Apologize. Do anything to stop her from retreating.

For a moment, earlier in the laundry room, she'd lowered her guard and let him in. But seated side by side now, she was pulling away again. All their mistakes cemented in stone filling the space between them.

Their boy had been kidnapped. The one person in the world who connected them, who they loved more than anything and would die for. This was the time they needed to not only present a unified front but to be united. If not as a married couple, then as parents.

"What do you have in mind?" he asked her.

"I want you to come somewhere with me, but you have to promise not to ask any questions until we get there."

"We can't simply leave without giving Tobias an explanation."

"Yes, we can." She searched his eyes, studied his face. "We've both done things to make it difficult to trust the other person. I get that, but I'm asking you to put your faith in me for one hour. Less. It's to help Ben. Please, Henry."

Blind trust in her had once come as easily as breathing, but desperation made people fools. It had driven her to hide the truth about the degree of danger she and Ben had really been in. There was no denying the part he'd played in that by filing for full custody. But now she wanted him to break protocol that was in place for good reasons, without him asking any questions.

"Allison." He shook his head. "I don't know."

"You can trust me and come along for the sake of our son. Or stay here. The choice is yours." Ally grabbed her purse and flew into motion, heading for the door.

His pulse spiked. He couldn't let her go alone. Anything might happen to her and stopping that headstrong woman from leaving wasn't an option. The divide between them would grow even bigger.

She was vulnerable and had asked for one thing. If he didn't give it, they'd be on opposite sides during this ordeal. She'd never trust him again, which might hurt their chances of getting their son back.

Bringing Ben home mattered most.

He glanced around. Tobias was in the kitchen, talking to another agent. The detectives were hunkered down in the dining room.

No one paid attention to her. The odds were good no one would bat a lash at him, either, until it was too late.

She was crossing the threshold.

Quickly, he caught up and shut the door behind them. "I'll drive. You navigate."

They climbed into his SUV. Behind the wheel, he started the engine, reversed out of the driveway and sped down the street.

"We need to get on the interstate," she said. "Take 805. Go north to I-5."

He headed toward the freeway, corralling his questions.

"How long until they notice we're gone?" She glanced back, checking their rear.

"If we're lucky, five minutes."

They weren't. Two minutes later, his phone rang, followed by hers.

"Ignore it," she said. "We'll deal with it when we get back."

He let the call go to voice mail and powered off his phone. "Tobias won't be pleased."

"I don't care. His children are safe at school right now, the way our son should be."

Quiet stretched in the car as he raced along the interstate, ignoring the speed limit. The air thickened, growing heavy with all the things left unsaid over the past year.

Allison had been the one to shut him out, erecting a wall of ice and a cone of silence between them. Not the other way around. The day she'd lost their second child, their miracle baby, a girl, was the day he'd lost Ally. But he didn't know why.

He was used to her hiding her thoughts and feelings, but this was different.

This concerned them getting Ben back.

Not to include Henry on the specifics of what they were doing felt cruel.

"Take that exit," she said, indicating the one for Del Mar.

He hit the off-ramp. "Where are we going? I think I've earned the right to know."

"Soon."

Patience was one of his strengths, but she was testing every drop of his.

Allison directed him through a posh neighborhood of mansions. Each luxury estate they passed wound the tension coursing through him tighter.

"There," she said. "Turn there. That house."

Set in an upscale residential area that only top one-percenters could afford, the *house* was more of a compound. Lights and cameras had been mounted atop a high brick wall surrounding the property. A Mediterranean manor was perched on a hill beyond a tree-lined path.

"Now what?" Henry asked, stopping in front of the iron gate.

"Hit the call button."

He rolled down the window and pushed the gray button for the intercom.

"Yes? How can I help you?" a male voice asked over the speaker.

Henry glanced at Allison.

She leaned over him and into the speaker said, "Allison and Henry Boyd to see Dante Emilio Vargas."

He gave her a shocked look.

"One moment," the voice said.

Had she lost her mind? "We can't be here."

"Why not? He took Ben."

"We can't prove that he's guilty of anything."

"So what? We don't have to at this point. All we need is to find out what he wants."

"This is a bad idea. We should leave." Accusing Vargas of kidnapping would only get them a lawsuit for defamation. "Follow protocol."

Exasperation flashed across her face.

But Henry wasn't reckless or foolish. They needed to be smart about this.

Allison crossed her arms. "Forget playing by the rules. You said yourself we need to get the negotiation process started. This is how we do it."

"What if you're wrong and it wasn't him?"

She shrugged. "Then we've lost nothing besides time sitting at home. But if I'm right, you'll have certainty. We'll get demands, and we'll be one step closer to getting our boy back."

Ally had been so fearless in dragging them here. Absolutely senseless. Henry didn't know if he wanted to kill her or kiss her.

The front gate swung open.

Henry didn't like this one little bit—Vargas, a supposed businessman, a pillar of the community and probable cartel leader, granting them access with no further inquiry, as if he'd been expecting them.

But he had to find Ben. In the absence of a warrant, knocking on Vargas's door was the fastest way to explore this possibility—and to validate or rule it out.

Henry gripped the wheel harder as he pressed on the accelerator, going up the paved path and around a large ornate fountain in the middle of a circular drive. Stopping near the stairs that led up to the house, he noted the guards around the perimeter. All of them were armed, judging from the bulges under their jackets.

If he asked, he was certain each man would be able to provide a license for a concealed weapon. As the head of a cartel, Vargas hadn't avoided incarceration this long by being stupid.

They got out and went up the stairs. A guard opened

the front door, letting them into a grand foyer complete with marble floors and a crystal chandelier.

Three guards greeted them.

"Hello, Mr. and Mrs. Boyd, I'm Rodrigo, head of security for Mr. Vargas. May I ask why you're calling upon him today?"

Henry looked to Allison. She was running this show.

"It's a personal matter," she said. "Will he see us?"

"He'll speak with Mr. Boyd, alone, downstairs."

"What?" Allison asked, not hiding the righteous indignation from her face.

"Mr. Vargas is in the sauna," Rodrigo said. "His schedule is packed. This is the only free time he has, and he didn't think you would be comfortable disrobing to have a conversation with him, Mrs. Boyd."

Allison balked, but there was nothing she could do.

"I'll speak with him," Henry said.

Another man in his midthirties with a trim goatee stepped forward. "I have to pat you down," he said.

Henry removed his Glock, handing it to Ally, and raised his arms.

The guy patted him down, doing a thorough job, going so far as to cup his privates. Then Rodrigo and a younger man escorted Henry down the hall.

"I'm Max. Can I get you something to drink while you wait, Mrs. Boyd?" the man with the goatee said back in the foyer, his voice carrying to where Henry was in earshot.

"No, thank you," Allison said.

Rodrigo opened a door to reveal a staircase and led the way to the basement.

They passed a wine cellar, drawing deeper into the bowels of the house. At the sauna door, the young guy directed Henry to a bench that had a stack of folded towels.

Henry went to the side and undressed, folding his clothes in a neat pile.

If Vargas wanted to have a private discussion, assuring the conversation wasn't being recorded, this was an excellent, discreet solution.

Wrapping a thick white towel around his waist, Henry gathered his thoughts. To help Ben, he had to keep a cool head.

Rodrigo opened the door to the infrared sauna and gestured for him to enter.

Henry crossed the threshold into the small room and a wave of massive heat enveloped him. Vargas sat on the upper bench, his arms outstretched along the wooden bar, his head tilted back, eyes closed.

Sweat glistened off his relatively fit body, rolling down his tanned limbs. If not for a slight softness around his middle and a sprinkling of gray at his temples, Henry would've taken the man for twenty years younger than sixty-something.

"Good day, Special Agent Boyd," Vargas said without bothering to look at him.

Henry climbed to the top and sat, embracing the hotter-than-Hades environment. "For the record, I'm not here in an official capacity and I didn't introduce myself as FBI."

"I'm very well informed. I believe your wife is a US marshal, if I'm not mistaken. What can I do for you today?" he asked casually.

"Our son was abducted this morning. We were hoping you might be able to help us get him back."

"I saw an Amber Alert. Was that for you?" His voice

filled with surprise. "I don't know what help I could possibly be."

"You have connections we couldn't dream of. Perhaps you could throw out feelers. See what turns up."

"I'm happy to try. Has the kidnapper contacted you?"

"No. But we're hoping to get demands soon. We'd do *anything* to have him home safe and sound."

Vargas lifted his head and met Henry's eyes. "Do you have any idea what his captor might want? Why he was taken?"

Henry got a sudden sinking sensation that he still didn't have all the pertinent facts. "No."

"I feel for you, truly. I have a son myself, although he's grown. And a few short days ago, my niece, Isabel, discovered that I'm not really her uncle but in fact her father." Vargas held Henry's gaze, his shrewd eyes narrowing, letting that tidbit hang in the air. "It was quite unfortunate how it came out. A man named Horatio 'Dutch' Haas, a US marshal, seduced Isabel, told her things about me that never should have been divulged, and now she's been spirited away somewhere. I fear I may never see her again, so I understand what it's like to have a child stolen from you."

The spit dried in Henry's mouth and he swore something slithered across his skin, but then he realized it was only rivulets of sweat.

"Perhaps, whoever took your son means him no harm," Vargas said. "Perhaps, they only desire what every parent wants. To be reunited with their child. If I had taken your son, which of course, I didn't," he said, sounding as deceitful as the day was long, "I'd want to hear from my Isabel within *four hours* and to hold her in my arms within *twelve*. Desires I'm sure you relate to."

Henry's stomach churned. Vargas was the most un-
conscionable, ruthless bastard. Henry had seen them all
in his line of work, but none touched this one.

"I'll mine the community, Mr. Boyd, using craft to
find answers for you. Stay tuned to every appropriate
forum."

Henry was missing something important in the conversation and wished Allison had been there. Vargas
had been careful not to let anything slip, but maybe he
could be rattled. "Thank you. We'd appreciate it if you
could hurry. It's come to our attention that the man who
is holding our son is known as *El Escorpion*. A hit man
for *Los Chacales* cartel."

Vargas raised his eyebrows. "That's disturbing
news." He clucked his tongue and wiped his brow with
a towel draped around his shoulders. "Scorpions are vicious. Those brutal pincers and their nasty sting can be
excruciating. Their venom toxic." Vargas pulled on a
distressed expression and shook his head. "I'd hate for
my seven-year-old to be in the hands of such a deadly
creature. Children are so fragile at that age. Like eggs,
easily crushed."

Henry hadn't mentioned Ben's age.

A vast hole yawned inside the pit of Henry's soul. A
chilling emptiness born of his deepening fears. Never
had he felt so impotent in his life.

"Good luck to you in getting your son back," Vargas said. "From one father to another, I'd recommend
ridding your home of agents and police. They'd only
impede the process." His voice conveyed a distinct
warning. "And be sure to give the kidnapper everything that he asks for. Without delay."

In the twelve years Henry had been in the FBI,

straight out of college, he'd killed to defend himself. Killed to save colleagues and protect innocent lives. But it was all Henry could do not to throw Vargas against the wall and pound his fists into him until the man stopped breathing. For the first time in his life, he had bloodlust.

But then they'd never get their son.

Swallowing hard, Henry tamped his emotions into the recesses of his heart. He got up, stepped down from the bench and pushed out of the blistering-hot room.

The younger bodyguard handed him his folded clothes and shoes.

Rodrigo was gone, replaced by the man who'd patted Henry down. He had a nick on his cheek surrounded by red skin, as if he'd been hit.

"Did my wife do that?" Henry asked.

The man grinned. "Indeed, she did. Rodrigo thought his temperament might suit her better, but I think she might shoot him. He's a bit of a sexist and has a candid tongue."

Henry hurried getting dressed, not concerned with modesty.

The two men escorted him upstairs into the foyer.

Allison stood rigid with a gun pointed at Rodrigo's head. Her arm was steady, her finger on the trigger, and her eye didn't waver.

Chapter Seven

Allison wanted to blow a hole in Rodrigo.

First, the one called Max had had the nerve to crack a tactless joke about how the tragic circumstance of their missing son would've made a good after-school special. Belittling her misery was hitting below the belt. Unable to restrain her impulse, she'd slapped him and her fingernail had grazed his cheek.

Then disgusting Rodrigo had raked his gaze over her body with blatant lust in his eyes, as though she were a sexual object, and topped it by licking his lips.

Well, now his attention was fully focused on the barrel of the gun in her hand.

"Hon," Henry said, easing up beside her. "We need to leave."

A soft touch on her arm had her lowering the weapon and removing her finger from the trigger.

"Ally. Now."

Face burning, she nodded, coming out of her enraged trance. Thank goodness, Henry had returned before the situation had spiraled into an utter disaster.

Her heart raced as they neared the front door and stepped outside. Passing two guards, they hurried down the stone stairs to the SUV.

"Did you learn anything?" she asked, hopping into the vehicle.

"You were right." Henry's grave tone twisted her gut into a knot. He turned the key in the ignition and gunned the engine. "Vargas has our son. I'm certain of it."

This was one thing she wished she hadn't been right about. Vargas was a contemptible man with no conscience. A drug dealer, murderer, kidnapper. He'd shed a lot of blood building his empire and there was no telling to what lengths he'd go to protect it.

Henry steered the speeding SUV down the path and out onto the road, the tires screeching on the hard turn.

Still holding Henry's gun, her hands shook. "Did he admit it?"

"Not in so many words. He didn't give me anything we could use to arrest him or bring him in for formal questioning. His team of lawyers would have him out before we got started. But it was him."

"What does he want?"

"Isabel."

Allison recoiled in surprise. "His niece?"

"Turns out she's really his daughter. He's livid the marshals seduced her, turned her against him and stole her."

His daughter? Her stomach soured. First, the marshals had harbored Vargas's lover, ensured she'd lived to testify against the financial firm laundering his money. Now, they'd meddled with his daughter. Convinced her to betray him.

Good God. This was bad. His hatred of the US Marshals Service was worse than she'd imagined.

"Vargas wants to speak to Isabel in four hours and

have her close enough to touch in twelve. That gives us until midnight."

The demand threw Allison for a loop. She hadn't known what to expect from Vargas, but it hadn't been that.

"Can you make it happen?" Henry asked.

"I don't know."

"Is she in WITSEC? Is there a legal obstacle?"

"Technically, no. But there is a logistical problem." A huge one. "Will and I thought it best to get Isabel and Dutch Haas, the marshal who did the seducing up in LA, out of the state and somewhere safe."

"When did your boss become 'Will' instead of 'Draper'?" There was more hurt than accusation in his tone.

She might've become friends with Will, but she hadn't discussed her marriage or Henry with him when they'd been out of town together. "There's nothing to it. Honestly."

Although there was doubt in his eyes, he nodded, letting it go. "So, tell me the problem."

"Isabel and Dutch are in Alaska."

"Call them. Explain the situation. We could arrange a flight and have her here in time."

"It's not that simple. I sent them off-grid, completely dark. No cell phones. No Wi-Fi. No radio reception. I wanted them to be untouchable."

"Sounds more like unreachable." He slapped the steering wheel, muttering a curse. "To complicate matters, Vargas wants us to get rid of everybody at the house."

"What?" She ruminated on what he'd just said. "Slipping out for an hour was one thing. How are we supposed to manage that? It'll be Twenty Questions with Tobias."

"We've got to figure it out and see that it's done. I think Vargas might have someone watching the house."

They were under no obligation to have the FBI or SDPD in their home, but asking them to vacate the premises, especially when Allison and Henry were federal law enforcement themselves, would raise red flags. Throw them under the spotlight of suspicion.

"I might have a way to get them to leave," she said.

"How?"

"Play the sympathy card. Pretend I'm an unhinged mother."

"That shouldn't require too much acting on your part." When she gave him an insulted look, he said, "You struck a bodyguard and pulled a gun on the head of security at Vargas's house."

"The safety was on." Her control had faltered, and she'd lost it, but if this wasn't an extenuating circumstance, then she didn't know what was. She handed Henry his gun and he shoved it in his holster. "The bigger concern is contacting Isabel in time."

Allison turned on her phone. Ignoring the ten voice mails that popped up on her screen, she dialed the number to Eielson Air Force Base in Fairbanks, Alaska. She knew it by heart from calling it so many times.

"Captain Williams."

She took a modicum of comfort from hearing the familiar male voice of the air force liaison she'd worked with to organize everything. "This is Deputy Marshal Chen in San Diego."

Henry let out an irritated sigh, no doubt at her dropping *Boyd*. Over the past couple of weeks, she had been trying to get used to the idea of no longer being his wife, no longer being a Boyd. It hadn't quite taken, and she'd found herself vacillating about keeping her name hyphenated.

"What can I do for you, ma'am?" Captain Williams asked.

"I need to reach Isabel Vargas and Dutch Haas as soon as possible. You wouldn't happen to have a way for me to contact them, would you?"

"No, ma'am. They've already left the base on their aurora borealis excursion in the Chena preserve. They'll be gone through the end of the season. Two weeks."

She was aware. Dutch had once mentioned wanting to show Isabel the northern lights. The remote location and Allison's idea to completely remove them from civilization had fallen into place. The 250,000-plus-acre wildlife preserve seemed the perfect place for them to disappear and figure out whether their relationship was real.

"It's urgent I speak with them. My son has been kidnapped."

"Oh, my God." Alarm tightened his voice. "I'm so sorry to hear that."

"Isabel and Dutch know who took him. I need their help to get him back. Please, if there's anything you can do, I would appreciate it."

"I'm sure I can clear it with my colonel to take a vehicle out there and search for them. I have a general idea of where they should be, but it could take a day or two. We're talking about a lot of land and you made it pretty clear that you wanted them to be hard to find."

Lori Carpenter had been the last person to betray Vargas. It had been Allison's idea to keep Lori up at Big

Bear Lake, almost two hundred miles from San Diego, even though Will had taken the credit for coming up with the secluded location.

Still, Vargas had found Lori and sent a pack of relentless killers after her.

This time, Allison had sworn to do a better job with Isabel. Not make the same mistake twice.

"I understand. Thank you, Captain Williams, and please call me on my cell phone as soon as you hear something. Day or night. No matter what time."

After she gave him her private number, he said, "I'll do my best, ma'am. Try not to worry."

She hung up, kicking herself for sending Dutch and Isabel to such a remote part of the largest state in the damn country. For Captain Williams, it was going to be like trying to find a needle in a haystack in the dark. It had been the best way to protect them, and it was coming back to bite her.

"It may take a day or two before we hear from Isabel," Allison said as something inside her deflated.

"Damn it. I got the impression Vargas wasn't going to be understanding about delays."

Maybe Vargas would take it out on her instead of her helpless child. Hopefully, Isabel wasn't the only thing he wanted and there was another way to appease him.

As soon as they reached the house, Tobias was out the door and on the stoop before they had parked in the driveway.

"However you decide to play this," Henry said, taking her hand, "I've got your back, one hundred percent."

Empathy flickered in his eyes, but it was more than that. Surety that they were united. His trust in her meant everything. It was nice to be on the same side, even if it was only temporary to get through this horrible situation.

"Thank you for coming with me to see Vargas," she said, soaking in his support like a dry sponge to water.

His smile was so gentle that it stole her next breath. "It would've been a mistake if I hadn't." He gave her hand a squeeze.

The gesture was small and warm, and shouldn't have been the least bit enticing, but she couldn't deny the shiver that ran over her skin. She was grateful he hadn't turned on her after she'd told him the truth earlier.

Henry's tenderness, his kindness, was one of his greatest strengths.

"Ready for this?" he asked.

She pulled her hand from his and smoothed back her hair. "I have to be."

They got out of the SUV.

Gearing up for the performance of her life, Allison stormed down the walkway with Henry behind her.

"Where on earth did you two go?" Tobias asked. "Why didn't you answer your phones?"

"I want you and everyone else inside our house to leave," Allison said as Henry stood beside her.

Taken aback, a crease formed in Tobias's brow. "What are you talking about? Standard operating procedure—"

"Save your breath," she said, cutting him off. "This is our home. Our son is missing. Not yours. Not theirs." Her voice broke on a choking sob. "I can't... I just can't have you all here. I can't breathe with you milling around. Your presence is suffocating me. I want you to leave."

"*We* want you to leave," Henry corrected. "We need some space to process everything."

Tobias shifted his gaze between them. "I'm not sure what's going on, but you both know better. I hope like hell you're not trying to take matters into your own hands and that you didn't go see Vargas. If anyone understands how dangerous that would be, it's you, Henry."

"If you won't make them leave, then I will," Allison said.

"I have to officially advise against this." Tobias shook his head, disappointment and confusion etched on his face. "If you're in trouble, if you've learned something while you were out, tell me. I'll do everything I can to help you. Did you go see Vargas? You don't have to acknowledge me verbally. Just nod. Have you been in contact with Vargas?"

Allison spun on her heel, flung the door open and charged inside.

"She's in a tenuous emotional space," Henry said to Tobias behind her. "We both are. Nothing more to it."

At her core, she was desperate, frantic, a step short of hysterical. Confirming Vargas had her kid only fired her up hotter and she was already in a pressure-cooker state. It didn't take much to release the searing emotions bubbling inside.

Allison stormed into the dining room and railed at the folks who were only trying to help them.

Once they got Ben back, she'd be the first to issue an apology, but until then, she continued insisting they leave, hollering her way into the living room, and going so far as to snatch a crystal figurine from the mantel and smash it on the floor.

She'd been storming around for several minutes, almost without taking a breath, when Tobias finally interceded.

"Hey, guys, let's pack it up. The Boyds will let us know when they've been contacted with ransom demands. Until then, we're not wanted."

They began to clear out and the scene of them hurrying to pack up blurred before Allison. Her pulse was racing and sweat pricked her skin. She tried to move, but the sound of her hyperventilating was so shocking to her ears, she froze.

Henry's gaze found her, his face tightening with concern. As if sensing she was spiraling and on the verge of coming undone, he wrapped an arm around her and shepherded her up the stairs to their room.

He closed the door and guided her to the bed.

She bent over, putting her head between her knees. With her lungs clutching for air, she drew in deep breaths. Fought the urge to really scream, voicing her helplessness. Not wanting to lose complete control, she clenched her hands.

Henry dropped beside her and put a hand on her back, rubbing in soothing circles.

"There's no way to get Isabel on the phone today much less back here to San Diego by midnight. What are we going to do?" A sharp sound of a wounded animal came from her. Tears fell from her eyes and dripped onto the floor. "What's going to happen to Ben when Vargas realizes we've failed to comply?"

What would that heartless monster do? The breath lodged in her raw throat.

Henry kept stroking her back in gentle motions, and she shuddered as the adrenaline began to drain from her.

"I don't know." He pried one of her hands open and interlaced their fingers.

She glanced up at Henry, whisking the wetness from her eyes. "Do you think he'd hurt him?"

"No, not at this early stage." His voice was steady, comforting, and she clung to the solid weight of his words. "Ben is his only leverage." He pressed a palm to her cheek, cupping her face. "Isabel could be half-way around the world for all Vargas knows. He must've considered that possibility." Dropping his hand, he grimaced.

"What is it?" The look on his face sobered her and she straightened. "What were you just thinking?"

"Things will escalate. With us being ready to do anything in our power to get Ben, he's going to up the ante. The next thing Vargas asks for will be bigger, more complicated. I fear it might be something ugly that we wouldn't otherwise agree to."

Chapter Eight

The first deadline passed. Henry and Allison waited, watching the clock. They were going stir-crazy in the house, dreading what Vargas might do.

Before long the sun was setting, and nothing had happened.

Henry hid his mounting anxiety behind a facade of calm though his nerves were strung tight. Allison checked her cell phone again for a missed call from Captain Williams or Vargas.

Would Vargas do something as pedestrian as call them?

He stared out the office window, his gaze trained on a black sedan parked two doors down across the street. Dodge Charger. Rear spoiler. The frame sat lower to the ground than usual. The windows had a dark tint, but through the windshield he noticed a guy sitting behind the wheel.

"There are no new emails in my work account or personal one," she said, seated behind the desk, typing on the laptop. "Do you want to check yours again?"

"I set my phone to vibrate if there are any incoming messages."

Ally sighed. "When you were with Vargas, did he say anything about how he'd communicate with us?"

"Nothing specific." He turned his attention to her and replayed the conversation in his head, filtering out his emotions. "Actually, he did say something weird. I remembered wishing you had been there to hear it firsthand."

She swiveled in her seat toward him. "What was it?"

"He's going to throw out feelers. Mine the community using craft to find answers. That we should tune in to every appropriate forum."

"That is bizarre. But it's not as if he'd say 'keep your phone handy.'"

"Not that he'd have to, though, right?" Folding his arms, Henry sifted through the dialogue in his head, like orienting pieces of a puzzle. "I mean, he knows that we're going to be glued to our phones, checking emails, watching the news. Even after Tobias and the others cleared out, Vargas has no guarantee that they're not still monitoring those channels."

"What other option is there? A note in our mailbox?"

"I wouldn't put anything past him, but that would be risky and a federal offense. He'd want something electronic, but hard to trace back to him, if not impossible."

"He's going to...mine the community using craft... Tune in to every forum," Allison said, repeating parts of what Henry had shared from his conversation with Vargas. She pulled the elastic band from her hair, taking down her ponytail, and raked a hand through her beautiful locks. "What kind of 'craft'? Why not just say he's going to ask people discreetly? Why use such complicated language?"

"Because he was talking in code." Closing his eyes,

Henry envisioned the words in his mind. There was a deeper meaning to them. Something Vargas assumed they'd connect to Ben and understand. "That's it!" Henry went around behind the desk and turned the laptop so he could type.

"Please, tell me what I'm missing."

Henry brought up the game their son was obsessed with. "Minecraft. It has an online forum that Ben is always sneaking into to chat with other gamers. I've told him it's not safe, but he's like you. Strong-willed." He pulled up the online Minecraft forum.

Sure enough, a private message had been sent to Ben's username from EnderDragon666 shortly after the first deadline had elapsed. Henry clicked on it.

I'm displeased I didn't receive a phone call. The next deadline is now 10:00 pm. A second failure will result in consequences.

A panicked chill settled in his heart. Vargas had moved up the deadline two hours. Not that there was any way they would've been able to get Isabel back to San Diego by midnight.

Experience told him it made no sense for Vargas to hurt their son, not when they were the only ones who could grant him access to his daughter.

"But how would Vargas know that Ben plays Minecraft?"

"When did the data breach happen?"

"A little more than a month ago."

"If Vargas has been planning to retaliate since then, he would've had the time and resources to dig into us, Draper, anyone in the office. It's not that hard to get remote access to someone's computer to spy on them. Did you get any unusual emails in the past month?"

"Nothing out of the ordinary."

"Did you click on any links embedded in an email sent to you?"

She brought up her personal email. "I wouldn't have opened anything from a stranger. I know better than it."

They reviewed her account, examining every email that hadn't come from him or an address belonging to a US marshal. Henry couldn't help but notice the abundance of messages from *Will* since they'd gotten back from LA. More in the past few days than past four weeks.

But he wasn't going down the rabbit hole of jealousy. Once Ally signed the paperwork in her purse and filed it, they'd officially be divorced, and she could do whatever she pleased with whomever. In fact, she'd been free to do so since she'd insisted on a legal separation.

It still peeved him she wanted a formal court order. The only reason she'd need that was if she was interested in dating without any negative repercussions in the divorce proceedings.

He glanced at the emails from Will again but dismissed them.

Allison wouldn't jump from one relationship to another. That wasn't in her character.

In the same way it wasn't in his to cheat. His father had run around on his mom and Henry had sworn never to do likewise. Not that he had ever been tempted.

Ally was the only woman capable of enticing him simply by breathing. Don't get him started on her smile, or laugh, or the euphoric rush that stole over him every time she walked into a room.

"I'll click on links in the school emails and from the PTA," she said, bringing him back to the task at hand.

He sorted those and scrolled through them. There was one from the PTA with a dot net address instead of the usual dot org.

"This one. I bet it's a phishing email." He pointed out the difference in the usual emails to her.

"How could I fall for that and be such an idiot?"

"You're not, Ally. Phishing can hook anyone. Add in the other factors of how busy you are, multitasking with a small child, and it's easy to understand."

"Do you think he's been spying on me through the computer?"

Henry opened the laptop settings and disabled the microphone and camera to prevent anyone from eavesdropping, just to be on the safe side. "Yes. I think that's how he knew Ben played Minecraft and chatted in the forums."

He forwarded the email to a guy in his office who worked on the cybercrime unit, asking him to quietly investigate it.

A car door slammed closed outside. Followed by two others.

"Who's here?" Allison asked.

Henry spun toward the window and looked outside. Three women were coming up the walkway, led by Karen Keogh.

Earlier when Tobias had told them to nod if they'd been in contact with Vargas, as soon as Ally had turned her back to go into the house, Henry had bobbed his head in confirmation.

It had been a split-second decision. He'd trusted Tobias to handle things discreetly.

But Henry hadn't counted on his boss and good friend sending his wife.

Karen was carrying a large baking pan covered with aluminum foil. Behind her was Rosalind Rodriguez, an agent from the office, also holding a dish. Bringing up the rear was…*Sandra*.

What the hell?

"It's Karen and couple of people from the office," Henry said, not wanting to start an argument or to upset Allison. "Why don't you stay here, and I'll handle it." He hustled out of the office, shutting the door behind him.

Just as he reached the front door, the bell rang.

He opened the door. "This isn't a great time."

Karen brushed past him, walking into the house without waiting for an invitation to enter. The other two followed her inside and he closed the door.

"Tobias sent us," Karen said. "He thought three ladies bringing you sustenance would be dismissed by anyone who might be watching. I heated up one of my famous lasagnas from the freezer, fried chicken and made the potato salad Ally loves. A home-cooked meal will do you both good."

Although Karen was a stay-at-home mom because she wanted their girls to have as much stability as possible with Tobias working long, crazy hours, it was beyond generous of her, especially on short notice.

"Thank you."

Karen and Rosalind made a beeline to the kitchen.

Once they were out of earshot, he turned to Sandra. "Why would you come here?" he whispered.

They were close and part of him was happy to see her friendly face, but Allison had the wrong idea about the nature of their relationship. Sandra was a wonderful person with a big heart, but he wasn't the least bit attracted to her. It was a coincidence she had red hair like his ex-girlfriend from college. Sandra was married, too, and they were both committed to their spouses. But Allison felt he had violated their marriage in some way with her.

He had no clue how she would react to seeing Sandra and didn't want to find out.

"I'm here on official business. Tobias insisted I come. But before I get to that, I'd like to speak to Allison. Alone, woman to woman."

"I don't think that's a good idea." As in the worst possible idea. This wasn't the time or place to resolve issues.

"What's not a good idea?" Allison said from behind him.

Henry spun around, feeling like someone had just walked over his grave.

Anger rolled off Allison in waves as she glared at him.

How dare this woman come to their house.

No doubt to comfort her bestie, Henry.

Allison was mad enough to claw Sandra's eyes out, but she had too much dignity to stoop so low.

Sandra handed Henry a Tupperware container. "He's worried about us speaking in private," she said in her syrupy Southern drawl.

Nails on a chalkboard.

"Why is that?" Allison asked Henry, seething.

He looked pale. He hadn't blinked, hadn't swallowed. Was he breathing?

"No reason," he said.

Allison shot daggers from her eyes at him, then smiled at Sandra. The woman was a total knockout. Bright blue eyes, long, fiery-red curls, an hourglass figure, her skin like poured milk. It was easy to see why Henry was drawn to her. "Let's talk in the office."

"Thank you," Sandra said.

Allison showed her to the office and closed the door. She gestured for the other woman to sit in a chair opposite the desk as Allison sat behind it.

Sandra flicked her hair over her shoulder, kicking up the scent of some sophisticated perfume, and settled her purse in her lap. "I'm sorry it's taken us so long to speak."

Allison wasn't, and didn't pretend otherwise.

"Let me start by saying that I'm the one who initiated a friendship with Henry. I only had the best of intentions."

Sure, you did. Allison silently nodded.

"That night in the bar, Henry thought you and I would meet and become fast friends."

They'd be friends when hell froze over.

"Three years ago," Sandra said, "do you recall hearing about an unnamed FBI agent that had to be hospitalized after a high-speed chase that resulted in a car accident?"

Once again, Allison nodded.

"That was me. What they didn't mention in the papers was that I had been pregnant and lost the baby."

Allison tensed. Sandra's loss was horrible, and she wouldn't wish such a thing on her worst enemy. But Allison didn't understand why they were discussing it.

"When you got pregnant the second time," Sandra

said, "Henry couldn't stop gushing about it in the office. He told everyone how you two were expecting a girl and that Ben was going to be a big brother. He was so excited."

"That's not true." Allison surged from her chair and walked to the window but stayed facing the redheaded liar. "Henry didn't want the baby."

Sandra blanched. "All I know is what I heard. Genuine happiness." She looked down and folded her hands. "One day, he stopped talking about it and started looking despondent. I was worried, especially since you had been far enough long to know the sex."

They'd found out the gender earlier than normal through bloodwork, noninvasive prenatal testing for certain conditions.

"I asked him if you were okay," Sandra said. "He explained you'd had complications and a miscarriage."

The memory pounced on Allison. The pain in her chest was unbearable, making it hard to breathe. Her legs grew weak and she was suddenly light-headed. She leaned back against the windowsill.

"That night, I consulted my husband," Sandra said, "and told him I was moved to share with Henry *and you* what we had been through as a couple. He thought it was a good idea. I told Henry first, but he didn't think you'd be receptive to hearing what I had to say. From there, we started chatting, and became friends. We only discussed things in the context of losing a child and the impact it could have on a marriage, the personal toll it could take. I'm sorry I overstepped my bounds. I meant no harm." She gave a disarming, apologetic look. "But I caused you unnecessary pain and stress. Then you two separated. I regret anything I did to cause that. My heart has been heavy over it."

Allison's eyes bulged and her throat burned. She had dealt with Southern sweethearts who came across as too good to be true, and had never trusted one. But Sandra was so straightforward and sincere, it was nauseating.

It was also hard to dismiss her as a manipulative liar when she seemed anything but.

"The healing process took me and my Nathaniel two years. But we're stronger than ever. I just wanted Henry to have hope. He loves you so much. Do you think you can forgive me?" Sandra asked.

The miscarriage had been the beginning of their problems in more ways than one. For Henry to discuss it with anyone other than a therapist was a violation. But after listening to Sandra, it was one Allison understood.

Ultimately, the veracity of Sandra's story didn't matter.

This boiled down to whether Allison could forgive Henry and believe in *him* again.

"There's so much going on right now," Allison said, "with my son missing." She didn't have the emotional capacity to deal with this today. "I need a little time to process what you said."

To think, she'd asked for a legal separation to give Henry space to see if their marriage was something he wanted or was simply afraid to lose because he had so much invested.

Allison didn't want him to settle for her out of habit, out of obligation. After the things she'd heard that night in the bar, she wasn't sure about anything. He'd been so chummy and cozy with Sandra, Allison had thought he might want to explore a relationship with her.

There was a knock at the door and then it opened. "Everything okay?" Henry edged inside the room tentatively, like he half expected to find Sandra strangled on the floor.

Allison nodded. "It's fine."

She'd blamed Sandra for quite a bit, but the woman's friendship with Henry had been a symptom of a bigger issue that had nothing to do with her.

"I guess I should get to the official reason why I'm here." Sandra stood, putting her purse strap on her shoulder. "Tobias informed me you two went to see Vargas."

Stiffening, Allison shot him a hard look of disbelief.

"I'll explain later," he said in an apologetic tone.

"I'm the handler for an undercover agent embedded in Vargas's organization. Code name Teflon. He's gone dark the past few days, no communication, but you may have encountered him today. If so, he might've tried to pass along a message. It's possible he might have proof we can act on that Vargas is behind the abduction. Did either of you find a note in any of your pockets?"

"No, but we hadn't checked."

Henry searched his pockets, as did Allison. There was nothing.

"Our suit jackets," Allison said. They'd taken them off in the bedroom.

Henry ran from the room. The sound of his shoes pounding against the stairs echoed in the hallway. A moment later he returned with a piece of paper. "I found a note in my jacket pocket, but I can't read it. Looks like gibberish."

"He uses a cipher in case it ever fell into the wrong hands." Sandra took the paper and pulled out a notebook and pen from her purse. Quickly, she scribbled in the small book, decoding the message. "I'm sorry, there's no mention of your son. No evidence we can use."

Allison's heart plummeted under the weight of the next deadline approaching.

"Damn it," Henry hissed, folding his arms.

Sandra's wide-eyed gaze lifted, bouncing between them. "But Vargas has asked his men to get him C-4."

Henry rocked back on his heels. "For what? Any mention of a target?"

"No." Sandra shook her head. "None. I don't think my guy knows."

"How much plastic explosives?" Henry asked. "A brick? Two?"

Sandra shrugged. "He says twenty-five pounds."

"Holy hell." Henry's shocked voice stilled Allison. "What on earth is Vargas planning?"

Chapter Nine

The house was eerily quiet as Lourdes padded barefoot down the stairs.

Most evenings, she'd have the television on and Javier would be blasting music while working out or playing video games.

Tonight, the stillness unnerved her. The forced silence was intense and electric.

Javier couldn't keep the boy and nanny bound and gagged in the guest room upstairs all night. They'd never be able to rest like that and there was no need for them to be restrained. Nothing inside the room could be used as a weapon unless they filed down the handles of the toothbrushes, but that'd take forever. The windows had a privacy tint to obscure the view inside the house and electronic locks, like the ones on every door, which Javier controlled from the high-tech security system.

Their two-story home in Ensenada was miles away from neighbors. It made her commute to school a slog, but her brother wanted to be able to see any unwelcome visitors approaching long before they were knocking at the door. The house was fortified to withstand a law enforcement raid. He'd even had a panic room installed in her bedroom and an escape tunnel built underneath the house.

Measures she'd dismissed as overkill before seeing firsthand the nature of his job.

Lourdes prayed this would be over soon. She'd told the school she was sick and would only be out for a couple of days. By day three, Principal Garcia would begin to wonder.

The delicious smell of hamburgers sizzling in a pan wafted down the hall, making her stomach growl. Her brother was a great cook and made a mean burger.

At the sound of Javier's voice inside the kitchen, she stopped cold just short of the threshold. Ingrained wariness had her pressing up against the wall out of sight. Before today, she never would've dared eavesdrop on her brother, but there was so much he wasn't telling her.

"Yes, sir," he said.

She peeped around the corner. Standing at the stove, he was on the phone, facing away from the hall. She ducked back behind the wall.

"Do you want me to wait until midnight?" he asked. There was a long pause. "I understand. It won't be a problem. No more mistakes on my part." He hung up and sighed. The sound of a spatula scraping against the cast-iron skillet sliced the air. "Lola, I know you're there."

Her pulse jumped and she hesitated.

Had he heard her? She'd been so quiet, so careful. Maybe he'd sensed her. When they were little, they'd been able to tell if the other had been near, hurt, in danger, in pain, sad, happy.

There was little point in pretending that she wasn't hiding around the corner.

Sucking in a deep, calming breath, she went into the kitchen.

He carried two paper plates with burgers and fries to the counter and set them down.

"Is everything all right?" She walked over to where he stood. "Are you in trouble because of me?" She looked at the blender in front of him.

He poured in milk and scooped vanilla ice cream into the mixer. "Don't worry about it." Grabbing the white drugstore bag he'd gotten after they'd crossed the border on their way to the house, he took out a medicine bottle. He unscrewed the top, measured out two doses of some purple liquid, and added it to the blender.

Putting on the lid, he started the machine.

As the concoction whirled together into a frothy white mixture, Lourdes's gut tightened.

Her brother wouldn't poison the hostages, drug them. Would he?

"What's in it?" she asked over the mechanical roar.

"Sure you want to know?"

No, she didn't and wished she'd never seen him add a special ingredient, but she *had* to know what the creamy cocktail was laced with.

Lourdes nodded. "Tell me."

Cocking a sly grin that had made many women melt, Javier shut off the blender and handed her the medicine. "It's all good. The pharmacist recommended it for kids who have difficulty sleeping. It's safe for him to take with his asthma."

She peered at the bottle. Melatonin—a synthetic form of the naturally occurring hormone that controlled sleep-wake cycles. Based on the dosage, Javier had exceeded the recommended amount a little, but not enough to alarm her. He probably wanted to ensure they were able to fall asleep with the adrenaline and fear that surely had them amped up.

Drawing in a relieved breath, she set down the homeopathic medicine.

"Only cut the boy loose. You might have to feed the nanny." Javier split the milkshake between two plastic cups. "I need you to make sure he drinks as much as possible."

Lourdes recalled how hysterical Tori had become after her gag was removed in the van for a few minutes. "I think it might be better if they eat separately. I don't want her upsetting Ben."

"That's fine. I'll feed her." He put a dollop of ketchup and a slice of cheese on the side of each plate. "I have to leave with the nanny after dinner anyway."

Surprise dragged her gaze to his. "Where are you taking her?"

"Back across the border." He set one paper plate, shake and straw on a tray. "Once they're both done, we'll eat together."

That was it? He wasn't going to elaborate.

They'd gone to the trouble of killing two police officers, kidnapping the nanny and kid, and threatening a group of innocent mothers in the park, all to simply take Tori back across the border? "Are you setting her free?"

Javier didn't answer, only stared at her with a blank expression. "You could say that."

She remembered what he'd told her in the van—the reason he'd needed her. "Do you have to send a message?" Her pulse skittered and her stomach turned at the idea.

"The less you know, the better." He handed her the

tray. "I can give you some melatonin, too, in case you want to sleep while I'm gone." His soft tone and sympathetic eyes made alarm spike through her.

She put the tray down. "Why would I need to?"

"I know how much you hate the lockdown protocol."

Ice water flooded her veins.

Under normal circumstances, she appreciated how he read her so well, anticipating her reactions, and loved his efforts to assuage her anxiety before she voiced it. But the way he was using it against her today, like a weapon, left her aghast.

The *lockdown* security function not only electronically bolted the windows and doors, but also engaged reinforced-steel shutters to seal them closed, blocking the Wi-Fi connection and cell phone signal. He was going to trap her inside the house with the child.

"What if there's an emergency?" She had codes for the basic operation of the system, but only Javier knew the master code to deactivate the lockdown protocol. Even if the sensors detected a fire, she couldn't override it. "Will you at least leave the entrance to the tunnel unlocked?"

"No." His voice was firm, his smile so gentle and sad that she wanted to scream.

Anxious energy bubbled inside her. She raked her fingers back through her hair, twisting the strands into a bundle over her shoulder. "Why lock us in? Don't you trust me?"

"I trust you." He pressed a cool palm to her cheek. "But I don't trust the kid. And once he gives you puppy-dog eyes and turns on the waterworks, you might forget whose side you're on. I can't have him getting into your head while I'm gone."

Her brother was going to trap her in a tomb. A luxurious tomb with a television and bed and every material comfort imaginable, but a tomb nonetheless with no way to reach the outside world.

Panic rose in her throat.

She swallowed hard, trying to tamp it down. "Javier, don't lock me in. You'll be gone five hours." *At least.* Maybe longer. "What if something happens?"

"Shh." He kissed her forehead and then met her eyes. "Just make sure *nothing* happens."

11:30 p.m.

HER BABY HAD been gone for fifteen hours. Dread furled in Allison's chest.

She tore her gaze from the clock in the lower right corner of the computer screen and looked up at the Minecraft forum. A blank chat screen stared back at her. No new messages from EnderDragon666, aka Vargas.

Just like Henry had predicted. *If we get another message from him tonight, it won't come through the forum.*

The cursor blinked, taunting her.

Sighing, Allison slapped the laptop closed. She shoved away from the desk, shut out the lights in the office as well as on the rest of the first floor.

She trudged upstairs and stopped at the doorway of Ben's room. Her thoughts whirled in an eddy of fear.

Was her baby asleep? Curled in the fetal position in a bed? On a cot? The cold floor?

Pushing the door wider, she stepped in. The stuffed red panda that Tori had given him, Sprocket, was on his pillow. Allison picked it up and pressed it to her face. Ben's scent filled her nose. For the first six months after he was born, she would hold him for hours at a time, smelling him, memorizing every inch of him. Even though her own mother had scolded her for it, warning that Allison was going to spoil him. She inhaled the panda again and her heart ached.

Was Ben wondering why his mommy and daddy hadn't come to rescue him yet? Blaming her for making his father move out and leaving him vulnerable? Did he miss Sprocket? Could he sleep without the stuffed animal?

Her gut twisted.

Allison forced herself to leave his room, carrying Sprocket with her. Inside the bedroom, Henry lay on his side of the bed, on top of the covers, fully dressed, shoes off. A lamp was on and he had a forearm covering his eyes.

He wasn't fully asleep. Only resting. He was trained to take advantage of the lulls in a crisis, even if only for ten minutes, to stave off fatigue so he was prepared when the time came to act.

Still, she couldn't wrap her head around how he'd been able to stomach the dinner Karen had made, with them not knowing if their boy had eaten. Or how Henry could shut his eyes and claim a moment of peace in the middle of this waking nightmare.

Maybe it was good one of them was able to set aside the living hell of the day and sleep long enough to stay sane. If only she could compartmentalize the way he did, breaking everything up into neat little boxes and tucking them away.

She sat on the upholstered bench at the foot of the bed, setting the stuffed animal beside her, and pulled off her shoes.

Her feet ached, but nothing compared to the anguish in her soul. Like someone had ripped out her heart and shredded it into a thousand pieces. She was afraid to lie down and close her eyes for fear the pain would consume her, but she was already in the clutches of despair.

Isabel was their one bargaining chip and Ally had squirreled her away in the far reaches of the wilderness where no one could contact her.

A howl of frustration rose in her throat, raw and deep. She bowed her head under the force of it. Covering her mouth with a hand, she muffled the guttural cry building. Fighting to hold on against the emotional tide. She clenched her other hand, digging her nails into her palm. The last thing she wanted was to wake Henry and have a total breakdown in front of him.

The shower. She'd let out her sorrow in the bathroom, the door closed, with the running shower to mask the sound, as she'd done many times before.

But then warm hands closed around the fist in her lap. *Henry.* He knelt in front of her.

She lifted her head, meeting his eyes. In that instant, all she saw was Ben. Parts of her son that no one else would see until he was older. With each passing day, Ben looked more and more like Henry and was taking on his mannerisms. Subtle changes only a mother would notice.

Gut-wrenching loss slammed into her. The loss of her baby girl. The loss of her marriage. Her family—the three of them together.

Nine years of memories assailed her, and it was too much. Too strong.

God, she couldn't lose Ben, too.

A deep sob racked her body. Tears she'd been holding back leaked from her eyes. Hot, stinging tears that threatened a torrent of weeping. Tears of guilt and stress and desperation.

This couldn't be real. This couldn't be happening.

Henry pulled her into his arms, but her heart constricted, her entire body tensed.

To let herself sink against him would break the dam, unleash the tidal wave, and she didn't know what state it'd leave her in.

He pressed his cheek to hers, hugged her closer, tighter. His chest rose and fell against hers. The solid weight lightening everything else around her. Then he eased back, turning his face toward hers, and their mouths were a shallow breath apart. His eyes met hers and she saw the same thing she felt reflected in his. Need. Desire for comfort. A yearning for the kind of connection they hadn't experienced in a long, long time.

But stark awareness scraped her bare. If she gave in for a moment, it would mean more than a kiss, more than a night of solace.

Rising, she edged away toward the bathroom. "I need to shower." With her back to him, she wiped the moisture from her eyes.

"Don't." The sharp command in his voice had her turning back around to face him.

"Don't what?" she asked.

"Run from me."

She stood still in disbelief. "What do you want? To see me wail? To show you how weak I am while you're this indomitable pillar of strength?" She loved that about him, steady as a boulder no matter the storm, but God, it was irritating at times. Made her feel as though she were coming up short.

"Weak?" He shook his head. "Ally, you're tough as gravel. So, do us both a favor and stop lying to me for once."

The accusation tore through her like a blade.

She exhaled through the silent moment, determined not to blink and push fresh tears to fall. "I do need to shower. That's no lie."

Henry surged to his feet, crossing the distance separating them. She backed up against the wall and he caught her by the arms, snatching her breath.

"Talk to me. Stop running and hiding what you feel." He huffed an aggravated sigh. "*Not* talking has led us here. To the separation. The divorce. Ben being kidnapped."

Resentment simmered between them, palpable and thick. But there was sexual tension, too, crackling beneath it like a live wire. Tempting her to melt into a puddle of mindless hormones whenever he touched her.

Before Henry, separating her libido from her heart had been simple. With him, the two were indelibly entangled, and sex had turned into a zero-sum game that she couldn't win.

He drew closer. His chest pressed to hers in the barest of contact, setting her alight, making her thighs quiver.

She hated how her body had never stopped craving his, reacted with such an immediate, visceral response. *Traitor.*

"Lean on me, angel," he pleaded in a tone that reminded her of the day they'd exchanged vows, had sworn to love one another until death. "Let me lean on you. Instead of using that damn shower as a smoke screen. You've done it ever since—" His voice died in his throat.

That was the kicker. The thing that burned her to the bone. He wouldn't utter *miscarriage* to her, as if it was a dirty word, but apparently, he'd had no trouble saying it to Sandra.

"Since what?" she asked. "Let me hear it."

"You know what."

"But I'm the liar?" She yanked back, trying to slip free of his grasp. "Isn't that the pot calling the kettle black?"

His fingers tightened on her arms. "What is that supposed to mean?"

"You've got some gall, Boyd." Her eyes stung from not blinking, tears beginning to well, but she'd sooner combust than cry. "Telling Sandra that you wanted our little girl when you and I both know otherwise."

His reaction was brutal, but gradual, like watching someone take a fist to the face in slow motion. Rocking back on his heels, he let her go. His expression turned so bleak and awful that her heart pinched.

He stumbled away and dropped onto the bench. "I... Why would you—" He broke off, giving her pause. Henry always spoke with such confidence, without hesitation. But now he looked flummoxed. Pained.

Even though he was kind and serious, wicked sharp and dangerously sexy, tough and protective—everything she'd ever wanted in a man—this was why she cried in the shower. Withdrew from his touch. Avoided the conversations that would escalate into arguments.

Because in the end, Henry didn't want to deal with the things he'd done wrong. He'd rather have them swept under the rug and forgotten.

But she couldn't forget.

He propped an elbow on his leg and lowered his head into his hand, as if he couldn't bear the weight of it.

"Do you really want to walk through fire with me tonight while our son is missing?" she asked.

If so, she was ready to burn and to set him ablaze right along with her.

Chapter Ten

Walk through fire?

He was in the eighth circle of hell, but he'd crawl to the ninth over broken glass and through napalm to get to the bottom of their problem. For Ben's sake.

Pretending, not talking, the pent-up anger simmering between them—it'd only hinder them in getting their son back.

On a selfish level, he needed to understand what had gone wrong. He'd signed those damn divorce papers earlier and had no clue how he'd lost his marriage to begin with.

Some obscure, slippery slope he'd tread upon, lost his footing and descended to the end.

When someone asked him why he was separated, all he could do was shrug and say, "Irreconcilable differences."

Didn't he have a right to know, no matter how terrible the truth?

"How can you say I didn't want our baby?" he asked, looking up at her.

Her eyes bulging, her jaw agape, appalled horror was written all over her beautiful face. "I remember your reaction when I told you that I was pregnant. Without

IVF, no shots, no stress. A miracle baby. You froze. I chocked it up to surprise, but the same smile and delight you'd showed over Ben never came. Did it?"

Henry swallowed hard.

Surprise was an understatement. He'd been shell-shocked. The one thing the doctors had said would never happen, could never happen, had. The impossible.

Propping a hand on her hip, Allison pressed her palm to her forehead. "The only response you gave was a woeful 'Wow,' like I'd told you I had cancer. Not a 'Wow! We hit the lottery!' Do you have any idea how disappointed I was? Feeling like we weren't in it together."

Once the news had sunk in, worry had eclipsed Henry's joy. "Your pregnancy and the delivery with Ben had been so hard on you. I didn't want you to go through that again."

She rolled her eyes. "As if you had any notion the degree of what I went through. I never told you about the pain, the constant nausea, the spotting even with the bed rest. The fear that seized me every time I thought I might miscarry. I didn't want you distracted while you were going through training. Fretting over me when you needed to focus."

Ally really thought him so clueless.

"You may not have told me," he said, "but I heard it in your voice whenever we spoke on the phone. Don't you think your mother filled in the blanks for me in ex-cruciating detail? And of course, she used that tone of hers that made me cringe with guilt."

Lowering her gaze, she winced as if to say she could imagine.

"I wasn't here as you were going through it. But,

hon, I was always with you. When you told me about the baby, I was scared and I freaked at first, but having a second child would've been a blessing."

Her head snapped up. "Is that what you told Sandra?"

Gritting his teeth, he sighed. In truth, he hadn't done much talking to Sandra. He'd mostly listened to what her loss had been like, how it had affected her marriage. As similarities arose, he'd confirmed the rough patch he'd been going through with Ally, acknowledged that he commiserated with the lack of communication, the distance, the unbearable silence. But he'd always followed it up with his love for his wife, his commitment to his marriage.

"I bet you didn't confide the things you said to me the day I miscarried. *It's okay. Wasn't meant to be. Ben's all we need.* As if losing our little girl could ever be okay."

Words to console them. Admittedly, a poor choice of words, but nothing more. "I was doing my best. We were devastated."

She scoffed as if she didn't believe him.

"When we lost her, I hurt," he said. "I raged. I questioned it. But I was trying to get us through something horrible."

Henry wished she'd let go of the mistakes he'd made. Not clean the slate, but give him the benefit of the doubt. That he loved her, that he was on her side and they were in this, as in everything else, together.

"I mourned the most heart-wrenching experience of my life *alone*," she said. "Don't sit there and act like you weren't relieved that day."

Henry hung his head. Demanding the truth meant this had to be a two-way street. "I was relieved," he confessed. "That you weren't going to endure another agonizing pregnancy confined to a bed like a prisoner. That I wouldn't have to face the possibility of burying you and raising Ben and another child alone if there had been complications. Relieved?" He looked up at her. "You bet. But that doesn't negate the grief, or the pain I also felt. You chose to mourn alone and forced me to do the same by shutting me out."

She didn't have a monopoly on feeling hurt and isolated. He felt like the biggest failure for not being able to get her to communicate even though they were partners under one roof, sharing a bed and a life.

Hot spots of color bloomed high on Ally's cheeks. "You were so devastated you waited a whole month to get a vasectomy, making sure we could never try again." Her voice rang of accusation. Betrayal.

Meeting her flinty gaze, he rose. "I didn't get the vasectomy behind your back. I told you to your face that I'd made an appointment."

"Without my consent."

"What if a man told a woman that she couldn't get her tubes tied, had no control over her own body without his consent?"

Silence dropped between them like a bomb.

She would've sacrificed anything to bring another life into this world, just as he would've given anything to ensure her well-being.

By not wanting to risk losing her, he did anyway.

His cell phone rang and he was grateful for the respite. He hesitated over the number on the screen before answering. "Boyd."

"It's Captain Roessler. I wanted to call you before you saw on the news that we found a body."

The statement hit Henry's gut like a wrecking ball. *Ben? Please, not Ben.*

"Not your son," Roessler said quickly. "It's the nanny."

Tori? "Are you sure?"

"Based on the photo and description of clothing your wife gave, we believe it's her. Her parents are flying back tomorrow afternoon. We'd like you to come down tonight and make a positive ID."

"Okay," he said, sounding dazed to his own ears. "Right away."

Ally was at his side. "Tell me. No matter how awful," she said as he ended the call.

"We have to go to the police station. They may have found Tori's body."

CAPTAIN ROESSLER LED Allison and Henry down the long corridor to the morgue. Allison's heels echoed in the hall.

As they entered the cold room, a distinct smell was the first thing to hit her. Formaldehyde and raw meat mixed with disinfectant. The room had white-tiled walls and floors, stainless-steel tables, and no windows. Classical music played softly in the background.

Roessler introduced the coroner. "This is Dr. Michelle Herron."

She wore a white lab coat, scrubs, latex gloves and Crocs. "Hello, Mr. and Mrs. Boyd. We'll try to make this as quick as possible for you."

Dread welled inside Allison and she braced herself. If Tori was indeed dead, what did that mean for Ben?

Harsh fluorescent lighting hummed overhead as Dr. Herron pulled back the white sheet covering the body and revealed the face of the corpse.

Pale skin. Vacant blue eyes. Dark red hair. A single shot to the forehead.

Shock washed through Allison despite her mental preparation. "That's Tori."

Poor Tori. An innocent victim in this madness. She'd been bright, warm, so vibrant. The young woman had been obsessed with red pandas, knew everything about them. Her boyfriend was planning to take her to the Smithsonian's Zoo in Washington, DC, to see some as her graduation present.

Now she never would.

Choked up, Allison looked away, around the sterile room. She focused on the glass-fronted cabinets and the tools inside. Various devices for cutting open bodies, other metal instruments and plastic face shields. There was a half-eaten sandwich on a paper plate on the counter a few feet away.

This grim profession required someone who was an expert at compartmentalization. Something Allison was struggling with since Ben had been taken.

"Thank you," Dr. Herron said. She covered Tori's face.

Captain Roessler nodded to the doctor and escorted them out into the hall. "Do either of you have any idea why the nanny was killed?"

Punishment for failing to get Isabel on the phone.

Allison folded her arms as guilt wormed through her. Tori was dead because of her, and now her son had no one looking out for him. Her stomach balled tighter.

"We'll leave the speculation to your detectives and the FBI," Henry said.

"Since you booted us from your house," Roessler said with a sneer, his eyes flat, "Special Agent Keogh is setting up a task force and an incident room in the morning. And Marshal Draper is sending a deputy to liaise."

Good of Tobias to keep the multiagency team together and on track. They needed all the help they could get, even if it was behind the scenes.

"Where was she found?" Henry asked.

"Five blocks from the police department. In a CCTV dead zone, but out in the open, where someone was bound to walk past her. It looks like she was killed somewhere else and dumped."

A clear, unmistakable message. Prompt, too.

Vargas was so adamant about keeping a strict timeline, he hadn't even waited until morning. He wanted them coiled tight with fear, sickened by their own helplessness all night long.

"By coming down, you spared her parents from having to ID her. I'll go notify them."

Tomorrow, Allison needed to call them and give her condolences. Apologize for dragging their daughter into her mess. She had their number in case of an emergency, but had never used it. That first call was going to be dreadful.

"Thank you, Captain," Henry said.

Roessler nodded and threw Allison an icy glare before he left.

She guessed he was going to hold a grudge.

"If murdering an innocent woman is the consequence for not giving that maniac what he wants," Allison said low, "then we find out what else he'll settle for and give it to him."

"That's a dangerous position."

"What's the alternative? We're talking about Ben."

Henry gave a heavy sigh and shook his head. "I don't know. Let's get out of here. It's hard to think with that odor."

She still smelled it, as well, and was more than ready to leave.

They climbed up the stairs rather than take the elevator so they could stretch their legs. Outside, it was quiet. The fresh clement air washed over them, but the stench of death was inside her nasal passages and clung to her clothes.

Beside her, Henry lifted his arm and sniffed his sleeve.

"We'll need to scrub it off," she said.

"Let's hope."

They got in the SUV. Henry keyed the ignition, sitting for a moment like he was thinking, and pulled out of the lot, heading home.

Traffic was nonexistent. The streets were slick from an earlier shower that had been short-lived.

By the time they parked in the driveway, it was almost two thirty in the morning. This was turning into an endless day. Pure torture.

Her head swam with worry and fatigue, but she doubted she'd be able to fall asleep.

They made their way into the house. There was no chime from the security system.

Then she remembered they'd been in such a rush to meet Captain Roessler that they'd forgotten to set the alarm. As Henry locked the door, she went to the security panel and tapped in the code. A ding sounded and the automated voice confirmed the alarm was set.

"I can sleep on the sofa, if you've changed your mind about me being upstairs," Henry said from the living room.

Not once in their marriage had he slept on the sofa. She'd thought living apart might give them clarity, but it had only amplified her doubts and muddied the waters.

Allison walked toward the steps, where she could see him. "I'm fine with you sleeping in our room." Solitude was the last thing she wanted. "But only if you'd be comfortable."

"I don't want you to be alone. I've never wanted that," he said, and the deeper meaning wasn't lost on her. "The master bath is all yours. Take your time. I'll shower in the hallway bathroom." Ben's bathroom decorated in a baseball theme because he was obsessed with the San Diego Padres.

Silently, they went upstairs and retreated to separate bathrooms. She stripped off her clothes, which reeked of the morgue. Exhaustion wore her to the bone, but she needed a shower more than she needed rest.

As soon as the water was hot, she stepped in under the spray. Lathering her hair with a fragrant shampoo that smelled of roses and vanilla, she stared at the marble bench seat. It had been Henry's idea when they'd renovated the bathroom to put one in. He'd envisioned a modern, spa-like space. A consolation for persuading her to buy the house she hadn't wanted. Henry was a rescuer. A good guy who didn't want anyone to be unhappy.

Job well done.

Though, he was right. She had started using it as a refuge. A way to avoid hashing out the tough stuff while using him as an excuse not to do it.

Since they were all talked out tonight—at least she'd hoped—Allison didn't linger. She toweled off and threw on her nightgown from yesterday. It wasn't provocative.

Soft cotton, simple, practical. It had straps and hugged her breasts but fell to her knees. She'd comfortably let Tori into the house wearing it.

Tori is always early. Was. She was always early.

Grief stabbed her and she left the bathroom before it got the better of her.

Henry was wearing a T-shirt and boxers when she spotted him slipping under the covers. "You were faster than I expected."

Was that a good thing or bad? She shut off the light and got into bed. "Sorry."

"No. I just thought you might need extra time in the bathroom, that's all." He rolled onto his back and stared at the ceiling. "I didn't want you to feel rushed because of earlier."

There was no way she could hide in the bathroom after what he'd said. "It's okay." She shifted her legs against the cold sheets, warming them. "Were you able to get the smell off?"

"More or less. How about you?"

"I'm not sure." That insidious odor lingered, but she didn't know if it was only in her head. She turned onto her side, facing him. "What do you think?"

He scooted closer and leaned in. Shutting his eyes, he took a deep inhale. A smile ghosted across his lips. "You smell great. The way I remember."

She considered him for a moment and had the urge to look away. But then his gaze found hers and she couldn't break the eye contact. She was in deep with Henry, a lifetime. Heart and body and soul. And it all messed with her head.

A thought sprang to mind, tickling her tongue. Contentious and incendiary, but she had to voice it. They'd come this far and had nothing to lose.

"I don't want to argue." She wasn't looking for him to take responsibility, only to hear her out. "I want you to know that I was angry, for a long time, that you took away our chance to have another child without talking to me," she said, realizing she was still holding on to some of that resentment. "Making an announcement wasn't the same as having a discussion. You didn't treat me like a partner when it came to a big decision that affected us both. I ached for the baby we lost and my heart hurt knowing we'd never have another."

Because of you. Though she hadn't spoken the words, they hung in the air, clogged her throat, filled her chest.

The worst part was that she'd buried her pain beneath seething anger, hidden it from him because, despite her indignation, she'd never wanted to hurt him. To see the heartache that gleamed in his eyes now.

He reached out his hand and took hers. Threaded their fingers. "I'm sorry."

She shuttered her eyes, unprepared for his response. Whenever she'd brought up the vasectomy, he went into HRT mode. Compartmentalized. Shut down his emotions. Stood his ground. Great qualities for hostage rescue, but that sucked in a marriage.

In the eleven months since he'd gotten the procedure, that was the first time he'd apologized.

"It wasn't until I was sitting in that crappy little apartment by myself for months, watching reality TV, that it dawned on me how I could've handled things differently instead of doubling down on feeling justified."

Henry could be self-righteous at times. Likewise, she could be obstinate, but the prospect of him indulging in reality TV threw her for a loop. He always poked fun at her for watching certain shows.

"I was worried about you getting pregnant again and carrying another child, but I could've suggested surrogacy. At the time, it didn't occur to me. All I thought about was keeping you safe. A vasectomy seemed the most feasible, logical, thing to do, considering you'd gotten pregnant without us trying. I didn't see another option back then. Thought I was right and had made the best decision for us. But the bottom line is that we should've decided together. I never meant to hurt you. I'm so sorry."

His sincerity resonated and a tear escaped her.

He cupped her face and brushed it away with his thumb. Warmth slid through her at the comforting touch.

More tears trickled from her closed eyes. She couldn't see him lean closer, but she sensed it. She soaked in the consolation of his nearness, the stroke of his hand along her cheek, the warm rush of his breath over her lips.

His arm wrapped around her, pressing her body flat to his as he held her. She burrowed against his chest. Drawn together by grief and fear for their son, and something primal, instinctual.

A part of her wished the sweet heat of his body didn't envelop her and seep into her skin, chasing away the shiver that had lingered since she'd seen Tori in the morgue. She felt the familiar tether to him, as though they'd always been connected. Always would be.

But was it enough to surmount their baggage?

Henry kissed her eyelids and cheek. Tender kisses spread across her jaw, and when his lips made their way to her mouth, she opened to receive his tongue.

A sudden hitch of a sob came from her and he swallowed the sound.

Too much had happened in the past year to be forgotten. Yet the longer she lay nestled against him, accepting his kisses, the easier it was to consider forgiveness for all the mistakes.

She didn't think he was seducing her or manipulating her, but that ease brought on from being physically close to him, being touched by him, made her feel malleable. Weak that he had such power over her and weaker still that she couldn't resist the comfort he offered.

With their legs entangled, chest to chest, the drowning kiss stole her thoughts, sent a jolt of electricity and heat through her, pulsing low in her belly.

She quivered as his hands roamed over her.

Her body hummed with sudden need, almost as if she were a tuning fork that had been struck. She vibrated with longing to share everything with him.

An intensity so strong, her heart throbbed.

The bed vibrated. The whole world buzzed.

He broke the kiss and pulled back. "Do you feel that?" he asked. "Is your phone in the bed?"

Leaning up on her forearm, she looked around. "No. I forgot mine in the bathroom."

Another muffled vibration rippled through the bed as a sense of foreboding rose in her.

Henry moved the pillows, tracking the sound. A cell phone she'd never seen before was in the bed. It'd been hidden in the covers.

Her heart skipped a beat at the thought of how it had gotten there. "Someone must've broken in while we were at the morgue."

That answered the question as to whether or not the house was under surveillance.

The cell phone buzzed again.

The sinister feeling inside her burrowed deeper.

They both sat upright, staring at the phone.

"Hello?" Henry answered, putting the call on speaker.

"You were warned there would be consequences," the voice on the other end said. Though it was more of a distorted hodgepodge of recorded words and syllables—both male and female, a variety of ages and accents—spliced together and spouted through some fancy software.

Vargas was using a voice modulator device.

"Please don't hurt our son," Allison blurted out. "I haven't been able to reach Isabel yet. She's off-grid. But I will. I swear it. I just need more time."

"Time must be earned," the montage of voices said. She and Henry shared a glance. "Tomorrow, at 9:00 a.m., you'll hold a press conference with every major media outlet. You will tell them you made a grave mistake by crossing *Los Chacales*. Let the world know it is only by the cartel's mercy that you live. But you must pay for your egregious offenses. The cost is your privacy, your anonymity. Yours and that of every US marshal in the San Diego office. You will name each of your colleagues, state their home addresses and personal phone numbers."

Allison's horror-filled mind raced at a frantic pace, like a mouse trapped in a bucket of water desperate to escape.

Henry looked at her, aghast. "What?"

"You heard me," the digitized voice said.

Inside, Allison screamed. She couldn't expose the identities of the other marshals in her office, tell the world where they lived. Make them and their families targets. Turn the USMS into a spectacle.

"Please," she begged. "There must be something else you want. Anything else."

"Reveal the new identities and locations of the three witnesses who have testified against *Los Chacales* at the press conference."

Her heart gave a painful clench. She covered her mouth with her hand and swallowed back a new surge of despair.

"The choice is yours," Vargas said, hiding behind that damn software.

"Proof of life," Henry blurted as if the thought had just occurred to him. "We want proof our son is alive and unharmed."

A pause. "You will get it. Then you'll have until 9:00 a.m. Fail again and there will be more bloodshed."

Chapter Eleven

Henry stood at the window, scouring the quiet street below for any sign of surveillance on the house. The muscular black sedan that had been parked outside earlier was gone. The car and the guy behind the wheel had been there when Karen had brought food, and as they'd left to go to the morgue, they'd driven past it. Henry had assumed it was one of Vargas's men keeping tabs on them.

Excellent odds that the same guy had slipped the phone into their bed. The thought of it made his skin crawl.

Now the man and the car were nowhere to be seen.

Something wasn't right. Even if the house wasn't under constant observation, they had to assume Vargas would want to remain aware of their comings and goings at the very least.

"For the love of God, what am I supposed to do?" Allison asked from the bed.

That was the ten-million-dollar question. Vargas had given her an impossible choice.

"You can't do either option," he said, clenching the phone in his fist.

Allison looked up at him. "He had Tori murdered a

few hours ago. If I don't do the press conference, who'll die next? Ben?" She pulled her knees up to her chest and wrapped her arms around her legs.

The air-conditioned vent overhead blew cool air down his neck, giving him a chill. Or was it fear, snaking its way through him?

He and Ally had each spent over a decade with their respective agencies, upholding the law, fighting for justice no matter the cost, even at great personal sacrifice.

And one phone call jeopardized everything.

How could they put one life over many others?

But they were parents first and foremost. How could they not do anything for Ben?

"Why is Vargas doing this?" Allison asked. "I thought he wanted Isabel back."

"He does." After the father-to-father tête-à-tête with Vargas, Henry was certain of that. "But he wants more."

"He wants to ruin me. Turn me into what he loathes— a traitor. Destroy my career."

"You can't do it." With terrorists, once you conceded, even a little, they owned you. There might not be a foreseeable end in sight. Not to mention the fallout from that outrageous demand if Allison went through with it.

"What's the alternative? We ID our son in the morgue next?"

Henry hung his head, slamming his eyes shut. Emotions burned through him. Regret, powerlessness, anger. A kid was supposed to grow up, thrive, follow their dreams and one day bury their parents. No mother, no father, was supposed to lay their child to rest.

First Tori. Would Ben be next?

"Vargas won't hurt him," Henry said with every drop

of confidence he could summon because Allison needed to hear it.

"You don't know that."

"Yes. I do." He opened his eyes and stared at the world through a haze of rage so dark and blood-red it clouded his vision.

"Vargas had that hit man put a bullet in Tori's head just to show us what he's capable of, how far he's willing to go. A twenty-three-year-old woman whose only mistake was being associated with me. The hell of it is, we can't prove anything. We have no evidence he's responsible for the kidnapping or the murder or that he's even connected to *Los Chacales* cartel."

Henry sat next to her on the bed, wrapped his arms around her shoulders and pulled her against him.

"Hon, you know Isabel. I take it she's a decent person with a good heart since you worked so hard to protect her. She's already aware that Vargas is the head of the cartel, that he's responsible for many deaths. Learning that he killed Tori would only spur her to see her father as quickly as possible to save Ben and help get him back home to us. Right now, Isabel has a compelling reason to talk to her father. But if Vargas deliberately hurt a seven-year-old child, what reason would Isabel have to see him? Would she ever speak to him again?"

Allison drew a quivering breath and pulled herself together. Her gaze shifted, and he saw the wheels in her head spinning.

"No. If she knew he was responsible, then she'd never forgive him." Ally looked up at him with both hope and renewed fear. "Never see him or speak to him again."

"This is Vargas's only leverage to get to her. Ben will

be okay." He had to hear himself say it. *Ben will be okay.* He'd keep on repeating it to himself until he believed it.

Vargas wanted his daughter back. The only way he'd alienate her forever would be as a last recourse. After he had exhausted every other possibility to hurt the USMS first.

"On the phone, he swore there'd be more bloodshed. If not Ben, then who?" she asked.

Henry shook his head, at a loss. "I don't want to find out."

"Then I have to hold a press conference. Nine a.m." Her gaze flickered to the clock. "In less than five hours. What am I supposed to say?"

His instincts pinged a warning, a gut feeling that kept him alive on hazardous missions with HRT. But he still couldn't pinpoint what it was.

He went back to the window and peered out between a crack in the curtains. "Why isn't someone watching the house?"

"What?" She shrugged. "Maybe someone is on sur-veillance and you can't see him. Maybe it's one guy and, after he planted the phone, he went to get some sleep, thinking we'd do the same."

Henry didn't like it. The break-in, the call in the mid-dle of the night, no one overtly watching them, turn-ing up the pressure. Something was off. It was wrong.

"I'm going for a run." He turned for his dresser and grabbed a pair of running shorts.

"Now?" Confusion etched her face. "We need to talk about this. Come up with a plan."

"We will." He got dressed, pulled on socks, sneak-ers, and threw on a warm-up jacket. "When I get back."

"Henry, this is more important than a damn run."

But his instincts screamed for him to get the hell out of the house and beat the pavement. Figure out what he was missing.

"I won't be gone long."

"You can't be serious."

"I need to run. Now."

His angel finally picked up on what he couldn't put into words. All expression drained from her face and she nodded. "Be careful."

He picked up his phone and keys and left the bedroom.

Downstairs, he swung by the built-in safe in the office and grabbed his Kimber Micro 9 Raptor. Unlike his FBI-issued Glock, the Micro was an easily concealed pocket pistol. Single-action trigger. Seven-round magazine.

After locking the door behind him, he took off on one his usual routes that led through Balboa Park. If they were under surveillance, Henry would flush the person out. The streets were clear at this hour, making it easy to spot a vehicle tailing him.

Heart racing, he powered across asphalt to the park. The path he chose would force someone out of a car and onto foot to stay with him. His mind combed through the details of the day as he pounded across the grass. It was like putting a puzzle together in the dark, only going off what he could sense. The crucial piece he was missing was almost within his grasp.

He ran in loops and backtracked several times to be absolutely certain no one was following him. Not by car to the park. Not on foot through the trails.

He came to stop in a patch of darkness and could feel his heartbeat in the hollow of his throat.

With dawning dread, Henry put it together. He figured out what he'd been missing back at the house.

He took out his cell and dialed Tobias.

On the fourth ring, his friend answered. "Henry, what is it?" His voice was groggy.

"Sorry to wake you, but our nanny, Tori, is dead."

"Are you sure it's her?" Tobias's tone came back more alert.

"We made a positive ID on the body. While we were at the morgue, someone broke in, left a cell phone. I think they also bugged the house and that's the reason they pulled overt surveillance. I wouldn't be surprised if there are also GPS trackers on our cars. And Ally's computer was hacked. We received a message earlier through a Minecraft forum."

"What do you need me to do?"

"We were given demands, but I don't think we can make a unilateral decision on this. Meet us, along with Draper, to discuss a course of action."

"Where and when?"

He opened his mouth and caught himself. Ally.

You didn't treat me like a partner when it came to a big decision that affected us both.

She'd resent it if he didn't get the okay from her first.

"Get dressed and wake Draper," Henry said. "I'll call you back with specifics." Provided Ally let him.

"Okay. I'll be standing by."

Jogging back to the house, he kept his eyes peeled and his guard up on the off chance he'd been mistaken and was indeed still under surveillance.

He stowed the gun back in the safe and took the stairs two at a time to the second floor. The sound of the television on low hit him as he stepped into the bedroom.

With her arms crossed, Ally sat up, waiting for him to explain, but didn't say anything.

He grabbed the remote and thumbed the volume louder. Taking her by the hand, he led her into the bathroom. He shut the door and started the shower to help mask their voices.

Pulling her close, he pressed his mouth to her ear. "I think the house is bugged."

On the run, he'd figured out that bugging the house made perfect sense. After Vargas had called them, he could eavesdrop to see how they were planning to handle things. Stay two steps ahead of them.

Ally stiffened in his arms. "What are we going to do?" she whispered.

"First, we'll put on a show for Vargas. Make a big deal about how we can't sleep in the house and want to stay in a hotel." Even if there were GPS trackers on their cars, they'd register under an alias so their room number wouldn't be easy to discover. "Then we're going to have Tobias and Draper meet us there."

She peered up at him with wide eyes and shook her head. "They'll never agree to the press conference," she said so low he barely heard her.

He brought his mouth back to her ear. "Four heads are better than two. It'll be easier to find a solution quickly. If we can't, then we have to give Draper a chance to protect anyone we might endanger. He can fire you, but he can't stop you from talking to the press. I think we need to sit down and talk to them."

Excluding them wasn't the smart play, but he and Ally needed to make a united decision. They had to be in agreement on everything moving forward.

She nodded. "I'll trust your gut." But her eyes told him that she thought this was going to backfire.

THE DREAM STAYED with Lourdes. Javier had returned, the steel shutters had lifted and the sun had risen. But dark tendrils of the nightmare clung to her like choking vines.

"When can I go home?" Ben asked, seated at the kitchen table, eating his breakfast of scrambled eggs and buttered toast.

Javier hitched a grin. "I don't know, buddy." His voice was light, friendly. "Hopefully soon."

Lourdes sipped her coffee, not missing a beat of the interaction between her brother and Ben. She was grateful the child was eating and hadn't shed a single tear this morning. It had taken some initial coaxing to get him downstairs and she'd had to turn on the radio. The boy loved music. It had a calming effect on him and had done the trick to get him through dinner last night. This morning he was more relaxed, less skittish.

"Can I go outside and look around?" Ben glanced at the window.

"Afraid not," her brother said softly, his expression kind. "Not much to see anyway. There's nothing around for a good mile."

"But there's a wind turbine," Ben said, pointing. "I've never seen one in real life up close."

"How do you know what a wind turbine is?" Lourdes asked. Most of the kids in her class would've called it a giant propeller.

"They have them in Minecraft. You can use it as a renewable energy source for electricity."

Her curiosity and surprise over the little boy suddenly threaded with fear when she shifted her gaze to her brother. The soft smile on Javier's face fell as he shot her a sly glance that spoke volumes.

The boy is clever. Don't underestimate him.

She remembered the warning. "It's best if you stay inside."

Ben frowned, lowering his head.

Javier blinked and the calculating look was gone, replaced by a practiced, jovial expression. "Hey," he said, far too casually, "that's why I'm giving you the freedom to walk around the house."

More like controlled access. The windows and outer doors were locked. There was no landline and their cell phones required a thumbprint scan to use. Javier had even taken the added precaution of hiding anything that could be used as a weapon by the child.

Everything seemed to be on track despite Tori's absence and Javier's lies to Ben.

"Are you sure Tori is all right?" Ben asked, looking up from his plate and setting his plastic fork down.

"Yeah, little man." Javier's tone was enthusiastic, encouraging. "I told you, I set her free."

"But why?"

Lourdes stared at her brother, eager to hear his answer.

"As an act of goodwill to incentivize your parents to cooperate." He pulled on a chummy grin, smooth and sympathetic. "So you can go home, too."

Lourdes put a hand on Ben's shoulder. "Do you know what *incentivize* means?"

Ben shook his head. "But I think I can spell it."

"Really? Let's hear it," Lourdes said.

"I-n-s-e-n-t-i-v-i-z-e."

"Ooh, real close, little man. There's a *c* instead of an *s*."

"But that was really good," Lourdes said brightly. "Do you like to spell?"

"I have to practice for the national spelling bee next month. Will I be home by then?"

Javier shrugged. "It's not up to me, buddy."

"Can I call my mom and dad? I don't want them to worry about me."

"I'm going to send them a message soon, reassuring them that you're fine." Javier finished his orange juice. "Let's be friends while you're here. Have some fun." He flashed a smile a cult leader would covet.

Her brother put on a convincing act, got people to drop their guard and lured them in, but then it hit Lourdes why he needed her. Javier couldn't maintain the pretense. It only worked in short spurts and the second something angered him, his true nature would crack through.

"You like playing video games?" Javier asked.

Ben nodded.

Javier leaned forward, resting his forearms on the table. "What's your favorite?"

"Minecraft." Ben shrugged. "It's the only one my mom will let me play."

"I don't have that, but I've got some others. You can choose between military dudes shooting it up or going on a mission driving a car."

"He's too young to play those," Lourdes said. They were rated Mature.

"I can dig out Fortnite. It's about survival and building stuff. Would you like that?"

Ben gave a hesitant nod, like he was trying to be cooperative.

"Drink your juice, get some vitamin C, and we'll go play, little man."

Ben drained his cup and followed Javier into the living room. They sat in front of the large-screen TV side by side. Her brother loaded the game and explained how to play.

Watching them together, Lourdes couldn't shake the nightmare from her mind or the chill from her skin. Maybe it was the way Javier only called Ben by a moniker—*little man, buddy*—instead of using his name. Or perhaps it was how her brother smiled with disturbing ease.

In her dream last night, Ben had been crying, screaming that he needed her, but he was far away. Lourdes had never felt that kind of fear, such abject horror. Javier had attacked someone. A large, dark figure that swallowed the space in front of her. A specter of a threat. She'd run to the kitchen to find something to help her brother. A knife. She'd grabbed the blade, but when she'd gotten close enough to the ominous shape, she'd turned and stabbed Javier in the back.

Lourdes shuddered, remembering it. Her blood ran cold. She rubbed her arms, desperate to warm her flesh.

Javier was her only family. The one person in the world who gave a damn about her.

She would never stab him in the back. Literally or figuratively. Never hurt him. *Never.*

After cleaning up in the kitchen, she shut off the music, grabbed a book and joined them in the living room.

Javier got up while Ben's attention was on the game. "Think of Spawn Island as a practice area. You can load up on supplies, but you can't take anything with you once you leave. So don't bother."

Her brother backed away from the screen and shot her a glance. The smile was gone, replaced with steely resolve. He raised a finger and pressed it to his lips, telling her to be quiet.

Javier took out his cell phone, brought up the camera, focused it on Ben and started recording. "Don't jump from the Battle Bus yet," he said in that happy-go-lucky tone. "Wait until the last minute, buddy. That way you won't have to compete for a landing spot."

"Okay," Ben said.

"You're a quick learner."

"That's what my mom says."

"I forgot to ask you, how was the dinner I made last night? Was it okay?"

"Yes. The burger was good. The shake, too."

"How about the eggs for breakfast? Were they tasty?"

"Yeah." Ben looked back over his shoulder and lowered the game controller. "What are you doing?"

Javier stopped recording. "Oh, nothing. I was checking something on my phone. Whoa, you better watch out." He pointed to the screen and Ben turned back to the game.

"What *were* you doing?" Lourdes whispered.

"I've got to send this video to my boss. It's for the kid's parents," he said, dropping the bosom-buddy affectation. An edge moved into his voice and his eyes turned hard as flint. "Proof of life."

The chill slithering across her skin sank down to her bones, and Lourdes realized she had no idea what the ultimate goal was of this kidnapping. Javier's boss wanted something from his parents. But what if they weren't prepared or able to give it for some reason? Then what would happen? Ben was an innocent child, a defenseless pawn.

"You'd never hurt him, would you?"

Javier's gaze didn't leave her face. "Like I told the kid, it's not up to me."

Chapter Twelve

Their one-bedroom hotel suite had a separate living room with sofa, armchairs, coffee table and a work desk. They'd booked the room under an alias and Tobias had agreed to foot the bill as an FBI expense.

Allison busied herself setting out the continental breakfast and hot coffee that had been delivered by room service on the table.

The smell of the fresh-baked muffins and croissants made her stomach churn.

"We need to explore ways to fulfill the demand," Tobias said, leaning back against the sofa and crossing his legs, "while keeping everyone safe."

"Fine." Seated in an armchair, Will emphasized the single word with a head nod. "Let's explore all you want, but it's not going to change the fact that we're faced with an insurmountable challenge."

Swallowing her frustration, she poured two cups of coffee and handed one to Henry, who stood by the window and paced in the confines of the small space.

Will took a large gulp of his coffee. "Even I don't know the new identities or the whereabouts of the three witnesses who testified against the cartel."

"It's for the best that you can't compromise the system," Captain Roessler said, filling his mug with hot brew then sinking back down in his chair.

She'd anticipated resistance from Will. His concerns were legitimate, but he understood her predicament. As the head of the San Diego office, it could've just as easily been him trapped in this situation with his kid missing. But Vargas had targeted her for some reason.

What she hadn't expected was Captain Roessler. Not only had someone invited him, but also he'd decided to back up everything Will said.

Allison set her mug on the work desk and pushed her hair back into a ponytail, securing it with an elastic band. "Vargas doesn't know where they are any more than we do. I could give false information."

Although, they were aware that Lori Carpenter had been relocated to Phoenix, Arizona. She was engaged to the marshal who'd protected her for a year, Nick McKenna. Nick's last day in the San Diego office would be next week. He was transferring to Las Vegas and taking Lori with him. In fact, the office was supposed to have a going-away get-together for him today.

"We would need to find Ben before Vargas discovers that Allison lied," Henry said.

"The cartel has hubs here and New York City, but they have people everywhere." Tobias added a packet of sugar to his cup and stirred. "We'd probably have eight hours max before they attempt to track down the witnesses and find that you either lied or they've been moved."

Maybe Allison should attend the luncheon, talk to Nick in person. He'd understand her dilemma and might even agree to send Lori to Las Vegas ASAP. That way she could offer Vargas her Phoenix address. Something verifiable and legitimate while keeping Lori safe.

"It would require a call to the attorney general to authorize disclosure of fake information under the pretense that it's real," Will said, "and I can tell you right now, he's never going to sign off on it."

"Rightly so," Roessler chimed in. "If you betrayed three witnesses on national television, false information or not, good luck trying to get anyone else to go into witness protection."

Will nodded. "We have a tough time persuading them to go through with testifying as is when they get cold feet. This stunt would make it impossible."

How would Will know about the challenges of massaging away a witness's fears?

She was the *closer*. The one in the pressure cooker who had to read people and sway them by telling them what they needed to hear. The job was tough, but it was all in the name of justice. She also did everything in her power to keep the witnesses safe.

"What about giving the personal information of the other marshals in your office?" Henry asked. "We'd work with them to keep everyone safe, especially their dependents."

"That would ultimately mean uprooting and relocating everyone." Will shook his head. "That's not something that can happen overnight, much less in a few hours. People have houses, children in school. Not to mention the impact to operations. We'd have to shut down our office for a week during the transition, if not longer."

"Good grief." Roessler scowled. "How can you afford to do that? Sounds like a move that'll obliterate your career, Marshal Draper."

Allison rolled her eyes. Would this man please stop stirring the pot?

This was the biggest mistake.

Henry had been so certain, so calm, about bringing Tobias and Will into the loop. He had a gift for homing in on critical details and seeing a clear course of action amid chaos. It was one of the reasons she'd married him. That, and he was *almost* always right. Almost.

With this, she and Henry should've handled it on their own.

"Hold on," Tobias said. "It's doable with the right coordination with the LA office. Maybe even some assistance from Sacramento and San Fran. We could probably limit the closure to a day or two."

"A day or two the bad guys win while the US marshals tuck tail and run?" Roessler asked as he took a croissant from the platter on the table.

Henry clenched his jaw, his cheeks reddening.

Will shook his head. Again. "That's unacceptable."

"We have to give the reporters something to report," Allison said, despair eating away at her hope. "That demand is nonnegotiable."

"Nonnegotiable?" Roessler repeated, diluting the word, undermining it. "I gotta admit this whole thing sounds insane." He was average height, medium build, a plain-looking, forgettable guy in his midforties, but he was holding center stage, dominating the room.

Every retort from him was a lethal blow, bolstering Will's position and widening the divide.

Allison regretted saying anything negative about the police officers who'd been murdered. She'd been terrified and frustrated and had lashed out at the wrong people, but this went beyond the adage "Don't speak ill of the dead."

Now Roessler was making her pay for it, without any apparent qualms that it came at the expense of her child.

"What Vargas really wants is to see Isabel, but she's unreachable," Allison said. "We failed once, and Tori died. I have to hold a press conference. The question is what to say to the press after I apologize for our *sins* against the cartel."

Will scooted to the edge of his seat. "Any kind of press conference where you apologize would be an embarrassment to the US Marshals Service."

"It would be a circus." Roessler bit into his croissant and wiped chocolate and crumbs from his lips. "The USMS would never live down the humiliation," he said around the food in his mouth.

Anger kindled in Allison. The slow burn tightened in her chest and spread up through her stiffening shoulders.

"Let's hear Allison and Henry out and give them a chance to fully explain their ideas before we shoot them down," Tobias said.

Will slammed his mug on the table. "The last time I checked, the FBI doesn't have to worry about the possibility of being neutered in front of the press."

Roessler laughed. "He's got a point, Agent Keogh. The FBI doesn't have a dog in this fight." He laughed harder. "Neutered dog."

"This isn't the police department's fight, either," Henry snapped.

Roessler set his croissant down on a napkin. "I'm

only trying to provide an objective opinion and help you see reason."

"You've been about as objective as an ISIS militant," Allison said.

"What?" Roessler sprang to his feet.

"It's true." Henry stalked up to him. "You haven't said one helpful thing."

"If you're upset with me, it's warranted." Allison paused and drew in a breath. "I can take it. I never should've disparaged two of your officers." Her apology seemed to take some of the steam out of the police captain as his chest deflated. "But what you're doing is hurting my son."

Roessler's eyes narrowed. "The way I see it, you and whichever corrupt deputy marshal responsible for your data breach hurt your son the most."

If the comment hadn't hit her like a sucker punch to the solar plexus, leaving her stunned, she would've done something she really would've regretted.

Tobias stood and raised a palm to each side of the room in a calming gesture. "Let's settle down, everyone."

"Who asked you to come here, Roessler?" Allison asked, her voice low and hoarse.

"I did," Will said, meeting her eyes. A shocked silence followed. "After Henry had a conference call with me and Tobias, explaining the ransom demands and asking us to meet here, I thought it might be prudent to have a neutral party involved."

Pivoting on her heel, she put her back to him. Will was a friend, or at least he was supposed to be, but he was up to something. He'd do anything to protect his career, his family, the office. She had no idea what friendship was worth to him, but he was doing every-thing in his power to torpedo her efforts instead of try-ing to help find an amenable solution.

Meanwhile, they were up against the clock. Time was running out. A decision had to be made.

Hang tough, munchkin. We're going to get you back. One way or another.

"It's already eight o'clock," she said. "I'm going to call the press and start setting up the press conference." Allison went to one of the hotel phones and picked up the receiver. She'd already compiled her local media list on a notepad.

"And what are you going to tell those reporters?" Will asked, coming up alongside her.

"I'll tell them I have something to say about *Los Cha-cales* cartel abducting a child. *My* child."

"As a deputy marshal?" he asked. She tried to assess his tone, but there was little inflection to his voice. Ev-erything about him suddenly felt walled off.

"Yes," she said.

"Then you're suspended."

Her heart flared and her mind went blank at those three little words.

"Effectively immediately," Draper added.

Henry had warned her that this might happen, but it still hit her like a slap to the face after everything she'd done. The only reason her son was in danger was that she was a deputy marshal, and a damn good one.

"I suppose, then, I'll have to do it as a civilian," she said, "who was wrongfully suspended. Thank you. I think they'll eat that up, and telling my story will buy me a few minutes of airtime. Not to mention I'm sure they'll get a great sound bite with me standing in front of the US Marshals building."

She stabbed the first number from her list on the keypad of the phone and waited for someone to answer.

"Hello, you've reached NBC 7," a bright, female automated voice said. "Please listen to the following options from our menu."

Will snatched the receiver from her hand and hung up. "Captain Roessler, please place Allison Chen-Boyd under arrest. Or is it just Chen? I can't keep track."

Roessler choked on his coffee and stood, taking handcuffs from his belt.

"What are the charges?" Henry asked as he crossed the room.

"Misappropriation of funds and wire fraud, for starters," Will said.

Allison reeled back. "You're lying."

Will went over to his briefcase, which was leaning against the side of the sofa. He opened it and took out several documents, holding them up.

She'd thought it odd that he'd brought a briefcase, but she had been so focused on everything else that she hadn't questioned it.

Henry snatched the papers from Will's hand and perused them alongside Tobias.

"These are documents requesting transportation and lodging for Deputy Marshal Dutch Haas and Isabel Vargas as well as payment for it," Tobias said. "Your signature is on everything, Will."

"I guess I forgot to mention forgery on the list of charges," Will said, his face unreadable. "I don't recall authorizing or signing anything."

Allison glared at him. "You're a damn liar! You authorized and signed everything."

"Are there any witnesses who supposedly saw me sign those documents?"

No. It had been over a weekend. Allison had been alone with Will in his office.

"Dutch and Isabel know the truth," she said. "Both of them heard you give me verbal approval to make the arrangements." They were the only ones who could exonerate her.

"I guess it's unfortunate that you've been unable to reach them."

"My son's life is at risk." Allison lunged for Will, but Roessler caught her by the arm and spun her around. Wrenching her arms behind her back, he slapped on the handcuffs.

She had the physical skills to stop Roessler, but some rational part of her brain still functioned enough to save her from assaulting a police captain.

Henry rushed forward to help her, but Tobias held him back. "Don't. You'll be sitting in a jail cell beside her and then who'll be able to help Ben?"

Allison's heart thundered and helplessness streaked through her veins hot as lightning. "Will, don't do this! My son could die. Please, I have to hold a press conference or there will be consequences." She struggled to reach him and shake a truthful answer from his deceitful mouth. "Why are you doing this?" she murmured, rattled by shock.

"I'm sorry." Will walked around and faced her. His expression was grim with apology. "But you know why."

Allison stilled. After spending almost two weeks

in LA with Will, having every meal together, listening to his anecdotes, digging deeper with the right questions, reading his body language, she knew why better than most.

He'd gone through an ugly divorce. His relationship with his wife remained contentious and she used every misstep on his part as evidence that he was an unfit parent. Allison also speculated that he had deep-seated daddy issues. All of which skewed his sense of self-preservation toward the extreme.

In hindsight, she should've realized that made him dangerous.

"Yeah, Draper. I do."

Roessler led her away, reciting her Miranda rights.

"You don't have proof I did anything wrong," Allison said.

"I don't need proof. Only probable cause, which US Marshal Draper just gave me."

"No district attorney will formally charge me."

"Not my problem or concern, and until then, you'll sit in a cell."

She could be locked up for twelve to twenty-four hours.

Henry rushed ahead of them and blocked the door. "Give me one minute of privacy with my wife. Just one."

Roessler's jaw hardened as he considered it. "Sixty seconds." He backed up, giving them a bit of space, but he didn't let them out of his sight.

"Maybe I could hold the press conference," Henry said.

"And say what? You can't speak for the marshals and you don't have anyone's personal information be-

sides Draper's. I don't think Vargas will settle for that."
Worry sliced through her.

"Is there anyone you can think of who could refute
Draper's allegations besides Isabel or Haas? If so, I can
take it above his head."

"His assistant, Lynn Jacobs. She might be able to
help. We didn't follow the usual protocol to arrange
things because neither Isabel nor Dutch was authorized
official protective custody. We did it as a precautionary measure. Lynn's number is in my cell phone, but
she's loyal to him."

"Time is up," Roessler said, coming over to them.
Taking her arm, he opened the door and shuffled Allison out into the hall.

"Ally," Henry called to her.

She looked back as he crossed the threshold.

"I'm going to get you out of there, hon. I promise."

Allison saw the fire blazing in his eyes. Henry was
going to fight for her.

She could take care of herself, but it was nice to
know someone else was looking out for her. When this
was all said and done, Will Draper would regret his
decision.

Chapter Thirteen

It was as if a claw tore at Henry's gut as Captain Roessler hauled Allison away. He slammed the door closed and marched deeper into the room. "I can't believe you'd stoop so low as to accuse Ally of a crime you know she didn't commit," he said, trying to stop his own spiraling guilt for bringing Draper further into the situation.

"If there'd been another option, I'd have taken it," Will said, standing his ground, "but she didn't leave me one. I have to protect the USMS."

Henry's stomach sank, leaden with remorse for thinking Draper would help. "Are you protecting the marshals?" he asked. "Or yourself?"

"They're one and the same."

Henry scoffed at that delusional statement.

"Will, it might be best for you to go," Tobias said. "I'll keep your liaison apprised of any essential developments."

Draper nodded, collected his briefcase and left.

Henry swore under his breath, frustrated with the catastrophic turn of events. "We've got to get her out."

"We will. But I'm afraid it won't be in time to hold the press conference."

A cell phone chimed. Henry checked his pockets. It

had come from the burner phone that had been placed in their bedroom. A different number from last time was displayed on the screen.

Henry opened the message. There was an attachment.

As Tobias came around to stand beside him and looked at the screen, Henry clicked on it and a video played.

His breath rushed from his lungs. *Oh, God.* "It's Ben."

"The proof of life you asked for."

His son was playing a video game and having a conversation with whom Henry assumed was *El Escorpion.* The man who'd killed two police officers and Tori.

A cold-blooded hit man was chatting with Ben like they were pals.

Henry replayed it, trying to identify anything that might reveal their location, but the video had been carefully filmed. Not a single shot of the windows, giving a glimpse of the surroundings outside. *El Escorpion* had stood at an angle where not even his reflection had been captured on the television screen.

"At least he's all right," Tobias said, putting a hand on his shoulder.

Abject relief gave way to dread. His son was all right…*now.* But for how much longer?

Vargas had been true to his word and followed through on consequences as well as giving them proof of life. While Henry and Ally were going to fail to deliver yet again.

He paused the video on the final shot and stared at Ben's face for several painful beats of his heart. *My sweet, perfect boy.*

His gut turned to ice. He sucked in a strained breath and his gaze careened.

Behind Ben, the television had frozen on a dark background. Something was reflected on the screen, but Henry couldn't quite make it out.

He zoomed past Ben, focusing on the TV. What was that? Not a face or a house or a building, but some kind of white structure. "Do you see it?" he asked.

"Yeah." Tobias leaned closer, squinting at the screen. "But I'm not sure what it is."

Taking out his personal phone, he figured a snapshot might be easier to analyze. He set the burner cell on the dresser, zeroed in on the screen and took a photo.

"Send us the picture and forward the video, too. You never know what we might be able to pick up."

Henry nodded in accord. Their tech gurus had sophisticated software that could freeze and analyze the video frame by frame. Forwarding it should've been his first thought.

He held a finger on the attachment. Menu options popped up, but most of the functions had been disabled. Forward, Copy, Save, Details—none of them worked.

"The SMS is locked down. Receive and Read Only," Henry said, adrenaline surging, his mind racing.

Without holding a press conference of his own, the next best thing was to call Vargas back. No way the guy would let him in through the front gate for another sitdown, but a disturbing thought hit him hard.

Henry brought up the number that had sent the video and put the phone on speaker.

"Are you sure that's a good idea?" Tobias asked.

"We need more time. I've got to tell Vargas that Allison has been arrested."

Tobias cocked his head to the side. "Do you think he'll care?"

No, but Henry had to try. He tapped the call icon.

An automated message played. "The number you have dialed is no longer in service. Please hang up and try your call again."

What the hell? Henry opened the call logs and gave the first number a try. The same message repeated.

"I bet he's using a secure voice over IP app that rotates the phone numbers," Tobias said. "Once one is used, he scraps it and moves on to the next. We can try to trace the source of the numbers, but—"

"Yeah, I know." If Vargas was using top-of-the-line software and presumably a talented techie, then a cell phone carrier had been hacked and an unending algorithm would bounce the trace to random recently disconnected numbers throughout the state. The FBI would be on a virtual wild-goose chase that led nowhere. "The odds are they'll be untraceable."

"Most likely, and any effort to decrypt it will take time."

"How much?"

"Minimum twenty-four hours. Worst case, days, and even if we're able to decrypt it, that doesn't mean we'll find Vargas with his hand in the cookie jar, so to speak."

Henry grimaced. "Did we get any kind of hit on the identity of *El Escorpion* or the woman who was with him?"

"Nothing so far, but we're still digging into it. Since many of the cartel's members and associates are from Mexico, I reached out to the Federal Ministerial Police late yesterday and asked them for assistance. Maybe something will turn up in one of their databases."

"Good thinking," Henry said.

"I'll make arrangements for us to set up in the closest possible room here. That way, if you get another call, we'll be ready. Everyone will have orders to ditch the suits and blend in as we come and go."

Henry nodded. "In the meantime, I'm going to see if I can reach Lynn Jacobs, Draper's assistant. See if she has any information that'll help get Allison out of jail."

"Honestly, I don't think Will has any intention of letting her spend the night in there."

"What makes you say that?"

Tobias lifted his brows. "Well, after speaking with him at length yesterday, I gathered that he's really quite fond of her. Believe it or not, despite that stunt he pulled. Besides, he didn't have just cause to suspend her and he knows that sooner or later the truth about his allegations will come out. I think he was desperate to stop that press conference."

"Maybe I should stand up in front of a gaggle of reporters and hang Draper out to dry. Tell everyone how she was suspended and arrested on trumped-up charges. Let Vargas know what's happening and why she wasn't able to follow through on his demands."

Tobias sighed. "That might do more harm than good. How do you know that won't decrease her value to Vargas? He certainly won't take pity on either of you. I doubt it will help."

Henry blew out an annoyed breath, hating their predicament. The stress was only mounting, and the day was just starting.

"Excuse me, I need to call Lynn."

In the bedroom, he found Ally's purse on the dresser.

He fished out her phone and scrolled through her list of contacts until he got to Jacobs.

Drawing in a deep breath, Henry took a second to calm his racing heart and settle his roiling gut. Then he hit her name and the green phone symbol.

The call went straight to voice mail and the phantom vise clamped around his chest tightened. "Damn it!" He nearly threw the phone at the wall, but he restrained himself, squeezing the cell in his hand.

"What is it, Henry?" Tobias asked, hurrying into the room.

"Her phone is off."

Tobias gave an unsurprised look. "Will Draper showed up here prepared to annihilate Allison's position. In case that didn't work, he brought documentation and Roessler as a fail-safe. Did you catch the captain's face when Will asked him to arrest Allison? *Roessler* didn't even see that coming. Now, if Will planned all that in less than two hours, don't you think he'd ensure that Lynn Jacobs would suddenly become just as unreachable as Isabel Vargas and Dutch Haas?"

Tobias snickered. "I'm starting to get the impression Will Draper is sly as a fox. Did you know that when a fox is caught in a trap, it'll chew off its own leg to get free? I'd advise you to watch out for him. I'll get someone to find Lynn Jacobs. Why don't you head over to the precinct, see Ally and show her the video of Ben. I'm sure it'd bring her some comfort to know he's okay."

Okay for now.

That sinking feeling would not let go of Henry. It wrapped around him like a shroud.

He stuffed Ally's phone in his pocket and took out the burner. Going into the messages, he wanted to see the video of Ben one more time, hoping it might assuage his growing fears.

But the text section was empty.

No messages. The video was gone, as if it had never been there. How? The phone had never left his possession.

"Henry?" Tobias stepped up to him. His expression was saddled with concern. "Are you okay?"

"The video of Ben. It's gone." His voice was low and raspy. "Like it had never been there." But Tobias had seen it. Henry wasn't so desperate that he'd imagined it.

"This is worse than we first considered if the message self-deleted."

"Worse in what way?"

"A remote wipe is an indicator that the tech being used is going to be harder to trace than I first anticipated. Virtually impossible."

Henry hunched at the desk. The weight of the circumstances pressed down on him, but he didn't have the time or the luxury to wallow.

Don't lose your head. Ben needs you. Ally needs you.

Squaring his shoulders, he rallied and pulled himself together. "I don't care what kind of tech Vargas uses. We're going to focus on the things we can control. First, dig up Lynn Jacobs from whatever hole she's hiding in so I can get Ally out of jail. Second, we need to track down the identities of *El Escorpion* and the woman who was with him. Analyze the photo I have of the video. They're the key to finding Ben."

WEARING LATEX GLOVES, Emilio sealed the last envelope on the desk in his office. He picked up the remote and shut off the television.

When the marshal had failed to meet his first demand, it had been expected. He imagined Isabel was on the other side of the globe, in Bora Bora or the Seychelles, undoubtedly with Dutch Haas. No cell phones. No Wi-Fi. Deliberately difficult to contact.

That meant the marshal was doing her job and, based on what he'd read in her personnel file, she was exceptional at what she did.

But to flagrantly fail to comply a second time caught him by surprise. She and her husband had sounded desperate to get their child back. So frantic after seeing the nanny's dead body that her becoming a turncoat had been a foregone conclusion.

Even though they'd gone to a hotel, where he could no longer eavesdrop on their conversations, they had given every indication they'd intended to follow through.

Yet, it was now two hours after the deadline and no press conference had taken place.

Looking down at the three envelopes, he smiled at the horror that was to come.

He welcomed this next punishment. The ghastly consequences would strike at the very heart of the USMS San Diego field office and flush out his traitor at the same time.

If Isabel learned of what was about to happen, he'd have enough plausible deniability to say his overly enthusiastic men got carried away and went too far with the bloodshed. That his sole intention was to elicit fear. Nothing more.

Not only would he kill two birds with one stone, but also the marshals would blame themselves for the tragedy.

It was his lucky day.

He pushed away from his desk, gathered the envelopes and left his office. Taking his time down the grand staircase, he watched Rodrigo, Max and Lucas chatting.

They all *looked* loyal. Said the right things. Induced his confidence.

But after Isabel—*his own daughter*—had willingly worked with the marshals and deceived him, anyone was capable of such betrayal.

As his men caught sight of him, they straightened and grew quiet, awaiting their orders.

Keeping his gloves on, Emilio strode up to them and handed each an envelope. "You are to open them separately. One is not to know the location or target of the others."

"Why, Don Emilio?" Lucas asked.

"It's a test," Max said flatly.

"This has nothing to do with testing you," Emilio said. "I assure you."

Glancing away, Rodrigo lowered his head. "He doesn't trust us."

Emilio peeled off his gloves and tucked them in a pocket. "I trust each of you implicitly." Everyone thought gangsters were always hardened steel. But there were times, such as now, when they were like temperamental children who had to be coddled. For one of the men standing before him, it was an act, but the other two were concerned Emilio had lost confidence in them. "There is simply no need to share the information. We must do a better job with our operational security. That's all."

Emilio ushered them outside with a wave of his hand.

On the veranda, he oversaw their final preparations. They each went to one of the light blue vans with a floral shop decal along the side and checked *the package* in the back.

The task was simple. Go to the location written on the paper in the envelope. Leave the van at the specified coordinates. The timers had already been set and activated. At noon, on the button, the explosives would detonate and everything in the vicinity would descend into chaos.

There was plenty of time for Rodrigo, Max and Lucas to flee the scene unharmed and without hurrying or drawing suspicion. Plenty of time for the traitor to notify the FBI and stop the explosion at his location.

They each opened their envelopes, read the paper, and all three shot him a questioning glance.

Then Lucas gave a two-fingered salute, hopped in and drove off first.

Rodrigo came around the front of the van and bounded up the steps to him. "Sir, are you sure about this?"

The one thing Emilio hated almost as much as betrayal was being questioned. "Absolutely."

Rodrigo's gaze flickered over to the extra blue van parked near the garage. "Why a fourth vehicle?"

"Merely a backup. In case something went wrong with one of yours."

Rodrigo looked down at the paper in his hand and up to Emilio's face. "If this is the target, I have to ask, did we take that marshal's kid?"

"The only thing you *have to do* is follow orders."

Rodrigo bowed his head. "*Sí, jefe*. Forgive me. I meant no disrespect. It's just this will bring a lot of heat our way."

Our. Emilio liked that, as if they were a team, but

he had a snake in the basket. He had to figure out who was truly on his side and this was the best approach.

There was no way in hell that any FBI informant or undercover agent would ever let a bomb go off without trying to prevent it. A bomb squad would be called in to dispose of it. The scene would be public and draw the media. Or the van would never show up at the prescribed destination. It would quietly disappear.

"Yes. It will bring heat *my* way." But he'd been forged in the fires of hell and, like tempered steel, was not easily broken. He could take the heat. "Let me worry about that."

"As you wish. We'll see that it's done." Rodrigo turned and hustled down the stone steps, throwing Max a hand gesture to move out.

Both men climbed into their respective vans and pulled off.

Emilio turned his face up to the sky and closed his eyes. Took in the warmth of the bright sun, the pleasant breeze brushing his skin, and thought of Isabel. The years of separation and lies. Of how she looked so much like her mother, more and more with each passing day.

He'd had an affair with his brother's wife, Maria. It was the reason his own had left him. Luis had suspected that Isabel hadn't been his, but then Maria had gotten sick. Metastatic cancer. The disease had taken her quickly. On the day she was buried, Luis sat him down and made it clear that Isabel was the last piece of Maria that he had left. His brother had recounted the judgment of Solomon from the Bible. Luis told him that either Isabel would be raised as his and all would be forgiven, or he would cut her in two like the baby in the story. Then there would be war.

Luis had drawn a line in the sand and Emilio had had to keep his distance from her. That had been the price for peace. For many years, Emilio had paid it, but war had been inevitable.

How could a father stay away from his child? His only daughter.

They had reached an impasse that only one of them would survive. Emilio'd had his own brother killed. Not for money. Not for power. Not to be king of the cartel. He'd done it to be in Isabel's life. To guide her. To mold her. To be the one who walked her down the aisle someday.

The marshals had not only forced him into a position where he had to tell Isabel the truth about her parentage, but also they had coerced her to turn on him and had taken her away. Ripped her from his world. Wanted to deny him any part in her future.

After the poison they'd poured in her ears, the odds of ever getting her back were slim to none. He had no delusions. Even if his original demand was met, Isabel wouldn't come running back to him with open arms and look upon him with the same love and sweet adoration he'd once cherished.

Yet, he still longed to see her, to hold his daughter one last time. As long as he had the little boy, Isabel would have no choice but to come. If for no other reason than to save that child.

Then at least he could tell her how much he'd always loved her, how she was the embodiment of his greatest hopes and dreams. To say goodbye to her properly— another thing that was taken from him.

He clenched his hands into fists. His brother's death would be in vain because of the marshals' interference.

Regret bled through him.

Opening his eyes, Emilio looked back at one of his new guards who stood near the front door like a silent sentry. The man had been brought in from New York and had no ties to anyone else here. "Go get *him*."

His bodyguard nodded and disappeared inside the house to retrieve Emilio's secret visitor who'd been killing time in the wine cellar.

Yesterday, Emilio had sent for a lieutenant from his division of the cartel in Mexico. The man had arrived earlier this morning, before the sun was up and unbeknownst to anyone else.

The front door opened. Samuel waltzed out onto the veranda, putting on his sunglasses.

Emilio trusted him, was impressed with his leadership in Mexico, and most important, Samuel didn't know Rodrigo, Max or Lucas well. There was no conflict with Samuel's allegiance.

"Do you have any questions?"

"No, Don Emilio. I understand what to do."

"As soon as you get there, leave. It's set to blow at noon, like the others, but you'll only have a few minutes to clear the area."

"Yes, sir." Putting on his gloves, Samuel made his way down the front steps and to the last light blue van with the florist shop decal. He hopped inside, backed up and headed out.

Rodrigo, Max and Lucas all had bombs, but with minuscule amounts of C-4 wrapped around bricks of modeling clay, which had a similar texture and color.

The detonation would shake the van and perhaps blow the doors.

It was only enticing bait. Nothing more. Emilio

couldn't very well hand a rat enough C-4 to bring down a building and send him to commit a federal crime that would be classified as an act of terrorism.

He was smarter than that.

Emilio shoved his hands in his pockets, watching the van with the real explosive payload cruise down the driveway and out the front gate.

He had gone to war once before and was prepared to do it again. To make the marshals feel his loss. To send his enemies a devastating message that couldn't be ignored.

No one messes with me or with what's mine without consequences. Not my cartel. And certainly not my daughter.

Chapter Fourteen

"What is she doing here?" Henry asked Tobias, looking pointedly over his friend's shoulder at Sandra.

She was settling in with a couple other agents in the adjoining suite that happened to be available. The living room had been turned into a command center. Their tech guru, Clifford Johnson, who everyone called CJ, was set up at the work desk, ready to attempt a trace on the next phone call with demands. At the moment, he was running the screenshot of the video through image-processing software. It would improve the quality of the photo, filter and enhance then analyze the details.

There was a whiteboard near the window with drawn curtains. On it were the photos of *El Escorpion*, his companion, the partial license plate of the black van and a map of San Diego.

Agent Rosalind Rodriguez was on the phone and Sandra was typing away on a laptop. Everyone was dressed casually in jeans and simple tops.

It was good to have support from the field office close by, but it was a very bad idea to have Sandra in an adjacent hotel room, especially while his wife was sitting in a jail cell.

"Is there a problem? I thought you two are friends."

"We are—were." Henry put a hand on Tobias's arm and guided him into his personal living room. "Ally isn't comfortable with us being friends."

Henry had never discussed the subject with Tobias. Whenever he'd tried while they were kicking back and drinking beers, in his head Ally sounded like an over-reacting, controlling wife, *or* he came across as an insensitive fool ignoring the possible pitfalls of a platonic friendship with the opposite sex. The truth was somewhere in the murky middle.

"I know you two signed the divorce papers yesterday, but I can understand you not wanting to upset Allison with everything going on."

"Actually, Ally didn't sign." Henry ran a hand through his hair. "We got the call about Ben and…" He shook his head. "The kidnapping has brought a lot of uncomfortable things to the surface. Forced us to have some difficult conversations. We've been closer in the past twenty-fours than we have been since we separated. I want my family, Tobias, and I don't want Sandra's presence messing that up."

"She's here in a professional capacity. She's smart and capable. Trust me, that's what you want right now, but I can ask her to keep a low profile."

A rap on the doorframe drew their attention.

"We found Lynn Jacobs," Rosalind said, sticking her head over the divide between the two rooms. "She's at her sister's apartment. Agent Dawes is bringing her into the field office for questioning. I told him to put her feet to the fire and not to let up until she told the truth on record."

Henry's chest loosened with an ounce of relief. He would take any shred of good news that he could get.

"Call Karen and have her prepare to unleash her brother," Tobias said, referring to his brother-in-law, a topnotch attorney.

"The SDPD isn't going to know what hit them," Rosalind said. "I heard he's a real shark."

"More like a killer whale who eats sharks for breakfast."

Rosalind smirked. "Also, I got you on the schedule to speak with the deputy director of the US Marshals Service. He's expecting your call in one hour and you'll have fifteen minutes."

Pride warmed Henry. He worked with some of the finest agents in the FBI. They understood the value of synergy, and would give their all to help get Ben back and Allison out of jail.

"Thanks," Henry said to Rosalind.

Tobias nodded. "Good work."

"No problem," she said. "I'm going to go over the surveillance feeds and statements taken at Chicano Park yesterday. See if the cops missed anything."

"Sounds good." Tobias turned to Henry. "We're going to get this fixed and Allison will be released. Even if I have to take this all the way to the Department of Justice."

Tobias might have pegged Draper correctly in that the man had every intention of having the charges dropped today. Though Henry appreciated that no one was relying on Draper to do the right thing. It was all-hands-on-deck and full steam ahead.

"Eventually," Henry said, "someone needs to clear the house of any listening devices. Also, Allison's computer was hacked. A phishing email."

Tobias nodded. "We'll take care of it."

"I've got something!" CJ called from the other room. Tobias and Henry both rushed inside.

On the sofa, Sandra sat speaking on the phone, engrossed in a heavy conversation based on the crease in her brow, but Rosalind joined them at CJ's workstation.

"What is it?" Henry asked, hoping whatever it was led somewhere useful.

"The program finished analyzing the photo." CJ indicated the snapshot Henry had provided, which was up on the first screen. "This is what the software picked up in the reflection of the television screen." CJ hit a couple of buttons and pointed to the three separate renderings on a second large monitor.

A leather sofa, the slope of a hill and distinct white rotor blades.

"A wind turbine?" Henry asked.

"Sure is," CJ said. "A large, three-bladed horizontal-axis wind turbine, to be specific. Wherever they're keeping Ben, there is a wind farm close enough for the reflection of one turbine to be captured on the television screen. Based on the angle of the sun and time of day, we can tell the orientation of the room in respect to the position of the turbine and approximate distance."

One step closer to Ben, but they still had a long way to go. "How many wind farms near San Diego?"

"I'll dive into that next."

"Sir," Sandra said, drawing their attention. She stood with her phone in her hand, her frantic gaze bouncing between Tobias and Henry. "My inside guy, Teflon, got an opening and called me. Vargas has deployed three vans with C-4."

The air in the room turned heavy.

"Where are they headed?" Tobias asked.

"My guy gave me his target and he followed a second van to its destination." She swallowed. "Sir, they're both schools."

"What?" Tobias whispered in horrified disbelief that was mirrored on the other faces in the room. "Why would he target schools?"

"Which ones?" Henry asked.

"Riverton Middle School and Morley Field Elementary."

"Morley Field is Ben's school." Why attack it when he'd already kidnapped Ben? "Hold on a minute, there's another kid we know who goes there. She's the daughter of a marshal."

Tobias swore. "What do you want to bet some other marshal's child goes to Riverton, too?"

After Tobias connected the dots, the name rang a bell in Henry's head, but he had to think for a minute. "Someone's kid in Allison's office does go there. She's been to a few basketball games to show support." He shifted into operator mode, fluid and filled with purpose. In total control. "Did your inside guy have any idea about the third location?"

Sandra shook her head. "All he knows is that the bombs are set to blow at noon."

"Do you know how many marshals have kids?" Tobias asked.

Henry wished Allison were there. She knew their names and schools by heart. "There aren't many kids. Six, I think, not including Ben."

Tobias stepped into the center of the room. "The names of their schools?"

Squeezing his eyes shut, Henry racked his brain. Ally was great about being supportive and showing up for big school events for her coworkers' kids whenever possible.

He opened his eyes to see Sandra standing at the whiteboard. She had Morley and Riverton already written down.

"Spruce Middle School," Henry said. Then he tried to recall the name of the school printed on the top of a Girl Scout cookie order form seven months ago. "Bay something. Maybe Bayview. It's an elementary. Siblings go there." He remembered Ally felt obligated to buy cookies from both girls.

CJ typed furiously on a laptop. "I've got it. Bayside."

Sandra wrote the name down.

"And Draper's son is the only one in high school. Gold Heights."

Sandra added it to the list.

"Do all the vans look the same?" Tobias asked.

"Yes." Sandra nodded. "They all left from Vargas's compound."

"Give CJ a description. I want an APB put out and, CJ, you need to tap into every feed in the city to find it."

"Sure," CJ said. "I'm on it."

"Where is your guy now?" Henry asked.

"He's headed toward Morley. He knows the area and plans to pull over near a field about a block away and attempt to disarm it himself."

Henry gave a low whistle. "That's risky."

Hostage Rescue Team only handled explosives for breaching doors and walls, but at a minimum, the members of HRT went through a course in hazardous device disruption. They trained for every contingency, but the course was nowhere near as comprehensive or involved as the FBI's bomb technician program.

"He won't have long to do it by the time he gets there," Sandra said, "but he's familiar with the type of detonation mechanism *Los Chacales* uses. He thinks this is some kind of a trap. A test Vargas is using to flush out his traitor. If my man gets burned, he's as good as dead. Teflon snatched the other driver off the street. He has him and the second bomb in the back of the van."

"Okay." Tobias clapped his hands and rubbed his palms together—a reliable indicator orders were about to start flying rapid-fire. "Teflon needs backup ASAP. Get our bomb tech and someone from HRT to him."

"What about Teflon's anonymity?" Sandra asked, looking out for her insider where others wouldn't.

"It's a sacrifice that has to be made. Only our bomb tech and one other will know. It might be best for you to head over there, as well."

Sandra nodded, backing down.

"I'll get on the phone with the school superintendent, tell him what's going on and issue an immediate evacuation of the schools. They can tell the students that it's just a drill. Rosalind, I want fire trucks dispatched to all the ones on the list. Even Riverton, if they can spare it, to keep up the pretense and cover Teflon's actions. Henry, reach out to your contacts in SDPD bomb squad. Explain the situation. I want a unit standing by for the third location when we find it. Get to work, people."

Henry gritted his teeth, hating that essential resources were being diverted from looking for his son, but Vargas had raised the stakes, and more than Ben's life was at risk.

I'M IN JAIL for a crime I didn't commit.

Allison sat in a holding cell, stewing. Roessler had

put her through the humiliation of the full booking process. Her vital statistics, mugshot and fingerprints had been taken, as if she were a common criminal. She looked around the bullpen for the umpteenth time. Large enough for eight prisoners, it had three benches, a toilet and a sink.

It could've been worse. She could've had company.

Captain Roessler came strolling by. She presumed to make another gloating pass to taunt her.

"I'm sorry about this," he said, standing in front of the bars with his arms crossed.

"No, you're not."

"No. I'm not. Just like, deep down, I don't believe you're sorry about disparaging my dead officers. You were only playing nice in front of the others because I kept busting your chops every chance I had. I prefer genuine hostility over fake niceness."

She stared at him, her temper flaring. "I should be out there trying to find my son, who was kidnapped, in case you've forgotten. Instead I'm locked up when I didn't do anything wrong and I think somewhere in that walnut-size heart of yours, you know it. If only you could see past the grudge you're holding."

His face flushed and he glared at her. "You should be thanking me."

"For what exactly?" She kept her voice cool, her tone under control.

"A couple of the guards joked around about putting you in that cell." He hiked his chin at the other holding pen with the women slated to be transferred to county in the morning. "They'd love nothing more than to take out their frustrations on someone in law enforcement locked inside with them."

No doubt that was true based on the way they'd glowered at her after Roessler's last pass when he'd announced her chosen profession.

Allison was silent. She was worried. But not in the way Roessler assumed.

She had taken Brazilian jiujitsu since she was twelve at her father's behest that she be able to defend herself. She'd parlayed her skills into a scholarship at USC and gone on to be a second degree black belt.

Her concern had nothing to do with those women hurting her. If anything, it was the other way around.

"Look," she said, getting up and walking closer. "I'm an angry mother, who is going to get out of this cell, sooner hopefully rather than later. When I do, God help anyone who stands in the way of me getting my son back. Because I will level that person. But I'd prefer if we weren't enemies, and that's no lie." She held his gaze. "What can I do to make this right? How about a donation to the California Peace Officers' Memorial Foundation in honor of your two fallen heroes?"

Roessler seemed to chew that over as the hot color drained from his face. Finally, he nodded. "And no more bad-mouthing any of my guys in SDPD."

"Agreed, though I am truly sorry for what I said. I lashed out at the wrong people. I shouldn't have disrespected officers killed in the line of duty while trying to protect my son. It was a gross error in judgment. It won't happen again." She extended her hand through the bars and he accepted the olive branch.

"We're about to place a lunch order from the deli down the street. Do you want something? A sandwich, soup? You've got to keep your strength up if you're going to be able to *level* anyone who gets in your way."

The sickening nerves that had been jittering in her stomach over the looming press conference had settled. With no access to her phone, computer or television, all Allison could do was wait, but without spinning herself up. For the first time since Ben had been taken, she actually felt hungry, as if she might be able to hold something down.

"Thank you, Captain. I'd appreciate that."

"I'VE PICKED UP the three vans after they left Vargas's compound," CJ said, pointing to surveillance feed he'd tapped into.

Henry and Rosalind gathered around behind him. Sandra had taken off to help Teflon and Tobias was still on the phone, making calls.

"At the intersections of Camino Del Mar and Fourth Street," CJ said. "And again, at Del Mar Heights and Mango right before hitting I-5." He rolled down to another monitor. "The first van had a head start of about two to three minutes. That's probably the one unaccounted for." He fast-forwarded through the footage, tracking the light blue van. "The driver took the off-ramp for I-805 south. Then over to 94 going west."

Rosalind dashed to the laptop in front of the sofa. "I bet he's going to Gold Heights High School."

Once the van exited Highway 94, CJ worked magic, tapping away like crazy on the keyboard, accessing the different camera feeds, never taking his eyes off the screen. "Bingo. I can confirm Gold Heights."

"Yes, Superintendent," Tobias said. "We have the third location. Gold Heights."

Henry turned to call his contact in the bomb squad and glanced at the first screen. There was another light blue van with a florist shop decal on the side, turning off Camino Del Mar onto Fourth Street. "There's a fourth van," he muttered.

"Huh?" CJ swiveled in his chair and rolled over to the monitor. "Sandra's guy must not have known about it."

"Let's track it." Henry hustled to grab his phone that he'd left on the coffee table. He redialed the extension he needed at the SDPD. "Hey, Pete. Gold Heights High School." He rattled off the address. "As a heads-up, we might have a fourth bomb."

"Holy hell," Pete muttered. "Four? I'm the only tech available at the moment. My supervisor insisted on sending our other guy to Morley."

"Why? I told you we were taking care of it with our own technician. That was a waste of resources."

"CYA, man. Nothing I can do about it. Listen, we're rolling out to the high school. En route now. ETA…five minutes." Pete disconnected.

Henry glanced at the time on his phone: 11:45. "Where is the fourth van?"

CJ attacked the keyboard. The clickety-clack sound filled Henry's ears, ratcheting his nerves. CJ frowned at the monitor, working faster than he had before, his fingers flying across the keyboard, accessing the feed from one camera and then the next.

The van exited I-5, taking Broadway, headed west. That wasn't far from their location.

"Where is he going?" Rosalind asked. "None of the schools on the list are in that vicinity."

A hard knot of doom tightened in Henry's belly. "The US Marshals Service building is on Broadway. What if he's…?"

The van turned south on Front Street, a block before the USMS building. Made a right on Market Street, going west. Then it stopped in between two businesses.

"What's there?" Henry and Rosalind asked in unison.

"Gimme a second." CJ chewed on his bottom lip as he typed feverishly. "Looks like there are two restaurants."

"Not another school?" Tobias asked, with his hand over the mouthpiece of the phone. "Are you sure?"

CJ nodded. "A hundred percent positive."

"Fast-forward to real-time," Henry said. "Make sure the van is still there and he's not waiting for something."

CJ did as he was asked.

The driver got out of the vehicle from the back, holding a floral arrangement, closed the door and crossed the street with apparent casualness.

"One of those restaurants is the target," Henry said, glancing at his watch: 11:49. Spinning on his heel, he made his way back into his room.

"Rosalind, call the restaurants," Tobias said on the move as his voice drew closer to Henry. "Try to get them to evacuate."

Henry grabbed his go bag. Every HRT operator had one with essentials in case they needed to respond to an emergency while away from the office. Then he headed for the door.

"Where are you going?" Tobias asked, following him into the hall.

"That van is a two-minute drive from here." Henry made a beeline to the elevator and hit the call button. "The bomb techs from our office and SDPD won't make it in time. They're on the other side of town."

The elevator chimed and the doors opened. Henry

stepped in with Tobias beside him and hit the button for the parking garage.

"So, what's your plan, hotshot?" Tobias asked. "Have you ever defused a bomb?"

"Does a simulation count?"

Tobias stared at him as if he were crazy. "No. It doesn't."

"Vargas has twenty-five pounds of C-4. Say he divided it evenly between the four vans, then there's 6.25 pounds sitting in that vehicle, counting down to take out innocent bystanders. I've seen half a pound detonated in a demonstration, inside a car under the driver's seat. It sent the roof of the vehicle twenty feet up in the air, moved the bulkheads and blew the doors. Now imagine the blast pressure of six pounds."

The elevator stopped and the doors opened.

Henry stalked off and jogged toward his vehicle.

"You could get blown sky-high right along with it," Tobias said, keeping pace beside him.

Henry's thoughts darted to Ally and Ben. He had to get his son back, no matter what. Being with them, having a future together as a family, was his greatest desire, but he had to shove it all away to the side. If he was going to survive the next ten minutes, have any hope of saving innocent lives, he had to turn his full attention on the immediate threat.

No energy could be squandered on personal considerations. That's how operators ended up dead along with the civilians they were supposed to protect.

Henry battened down his focus on the task before him. "How long do you think it will take Rosalind to get the restaurant owner on the line and convince them the threat is credible and to evacuate during the lunch rush?"

"I don't know. Ten minutes. Maybe fifteen."

"We have eight." He hit Unlock on his key fob. "If I don't try to stop that bomb," he said, flashing his friend a dire look, "who will?"

Chapter Fifteen

Henry was in luck.

The back door to the van was unlocked. If he hadn't seen the way the driver had gotten out, quickly and carelessly, then he would've been cautious of booby traps that might have triggered the bomb prematurely.

Henry opened the door, peered in and froze.

Eighteen bricks of plastic explosives were stacked inside. A formidable amount of C-4 wired to a timer detonation mechanism.

"Eighteen," he muttered, climbing into the back.

"Eighteen pounds," Tobias said. "Good grief."

"No." Henry unzipped his go bag. "Eighteen bricks means 22.5 pounds." Set to blow in the middle of downtown.

Vargas's need for vengeance knew no bounds.

There were less than seven minutes left on the timer. The pressure on Henry was immense. With his mind racing, he settled his breathing.

"Do you need help?" Tobias asked.

Yes, Henry did, but over Tobias's shoulder he noticed one restaurant clearing out, people sauntering onto the sidewalk rather than running for dear life. "You better go inside the second restaurant and get those people out of there. Make them understand the gravity of the situation. Everything within fifty yards of this van needs to be evacuated."

But there wasn't enough time. If he couldn't disarm it, a lot of people were going to die.

"All right," Tobias said. "But I'll be back. I won't leave you on your own."

Karen would have a ton to say about that.

As Tobias disappeared around the van, heading for the restaurant, Henry found his cell phone and dialed the bomb tech on their hostage rescue team.

Five rings and Valentine answered. "We're still breathing. Yahoo!"

"Thank God." Henry's pulse drummed in his ear as he put the call on speaker and set the phone down. "I have a fourth bomb. Eighteen bricks. I need an assist defusing."

Valentine whistled low. "You got the mother lode," he said, full of excitement only a bomb tech could appreciate. "We had a trifling amount. I did a controlled detonation of one of ours for optics. We had to sell it for Teflon. I take it you've got the same detonation mechanism but tell me what you see to be sure."

Henry described the detonator down to wire color and stared at the red timer counting down. "I have five minutes, forty seconds. Do you read me?" Heart palpitating at a frantic beat, he wiped his palms on his jeans and took a deep breath.

"Roger," Valentine said over the line. "Don't freak out, but your detonator is different than what I had. A lot more wires. Tell me you have your go bag and your kit."

"Yep." Henry unzipped his bag and fished out the black kit. It shook in his trembling hands. Inside were tweezers, mini clamps and a pair of small scissors. "Now what?"

"Take off the front plate of the timer." Valentine's voice was smooth gravel. "I need to know how the wiring is connected inside."

Henry glanced at the timer. "Five minutes." Time was running out way too fast, but he couldn't let this bomb go off. He took out the mini screwdriver from the kit and started removing the front plastic cover.

Determination rippled through him in a wave of frost. He had to do this. For every person in the vicinity who would become collateral damage. For his wife. For his son. He'd made promises to be there for them and intended to keep them.

A sense of calm detachment came over him as he loosened two screws on the cover and then worked on the other two.

"Time check," Valentine said, calm in his ear.

The last screw fell out. Henry flipped off the plastic cover, letting it hit the van floor. "Four minutes, ten seconds." He told Valentine about the inner connections and how everything was wired to the timer.

"We have to start disarming it now. It'll be tricky, but I'll walk you through it. Hope you've got steady hands."

Right on cue, Henry's hand quivered. *Damn it.*

"You're going to clamp most of the wires together, off to the side," Valentine said through the speaker. "Except for the blue and red ones. Leave those free."

Beaded sweat on Henry's forehead rolled down the bridge of his nose. The van was a good ten degrees hotter than it was outside. He wished the air conditioner were on as the air was stifling. He looked over the wires to follow Valentine's instructions.

Red, yellow, green, orange, black, white, black. *What?*

"There are two black wires. I never said blue." He checked the wires again. "Valentine, do you copy? There are two black wires."

"That's not right. There should be a blue one."

Henry tried to swallow. His mouth and throat went desert dry. "Are you sure? What if there are two black?"

"Then you're hosed."

Rifling through his bag, he searched his gear by touch-looking for his mini flashlight. When he found it, he turned it on and scanned over the device. Red, yellow, black, green, white, orange…dark blue. "Got it."

How was he going to hold the flashlight, use the clamps and cut the wires?

As he considered putting the light in his mouth and essentially taking away his ability to communicate, Tobias appeared at the back of the van and opened the door wide. Gathering around him were Will Draper, Nick McKenna and several other marshals.

They must've been the targets inside the restaurant. But Henry didn't have the bandwidth to speculate how Vargas knew they'd be there. He'd deal with that later.

"What can we do?" Tobias asked.

"I need someone to shine the light here," Henry said. "Everyone else can help clear out the area. We've got three minutes left."

Tobias took the flashlight and the others leaped into action.

"Thank you," Henry said. A fissure of hope cracked the tightness constricting his chest. He licked his lips, but his parched tongue might as well have been sandpaper. Clamping the white and green wires, he said. "I need tweezers."

Tobias handed him the tool from the kit.

Holding the instrument in his right hand, he delicately pulled the yellow and orange wires to the side and clipped them. "The black wire is tangled around the red one. The others are clamped."

"Is the blue free?"

"Yes," Henry confirmed.

"Do what you can to separate the black and red wires. You just need enough space to cut the red one without snipping the black," Valentine said. "But don't cut it until I say so and you need to hurry."

That went without saying. *Two minutes, thirty seconds.*

Droplets of sweat dripped onto the bricks of C-4 and the circuity of the timer. A crackling sizzle emitted. A puff of smoke curled up.

Henry's heart skittered and he glanced at Tobias, who grimaced.

"Time check?" Valentine asked.

"Two minutes, ten seconds," Tobias said,

"Moisture hit the circuit board." Henry wiped his forehead with a wrist.

"Not good," Valentine said. "If it short-circuits, it'll detonate."

A block of ice dropped in Henry's gut. He wiped his hands on his thighs, sucking in a breath to steady himself, and pulled out another clamp from the kit.

The red wire was twisted around the black. Using the tweezers and a clamp, he gently plucked the black one and eased it to the side for enough separation.

"Hold the clamp," he said to Tobias, who took it. After letting out a steady exhale, he said, "Okay, Valentine. What's next?"

"Do-or-die time, man. Cut the blue first, then the red," Valentine instructed.

Henry slipped the small scissors from the case.

"Something you should know," Valentine added. "Once you cut the blue wire, the countdown will accelerate. Cut the red wire as fast as you can to stop it. Time check?"

"One minute, thirty seconds," Tobias said to Valentine without blinking.

Adrenaline hummed in Henry's veins, tension tightening through his shoulder blades. Keeping his hand steady, he positioned the scissors around the blue wire. "Keep your eyes on the timer," he said to Tobias, "and me up to speed on where we stand. Let me know when you're ready."

"Go."

Henry snipped the blue wire.

"One minute."

Damn, that escalated quickly.

Twisting his hand, Henry tried to angle the blades in between the red and black wires, but there was less space than he'd estimated.

"Forty seconds," Tobias snapped, impatience and nerves getting the best of him.

Nausea inundated Henry's system, but he didn't focus on it. He wiggled the tip of the closed tweezers in between the two wires and spread them apart a bit more.

"Thirty seconds."

The scissors slipped from Henry's damp fingers as his throbbing heart did a backflip into his throat. He fumbled for them, grabbing the scissors from the van floor.

"Twenty seconds."

Keeping the wires separated with the tweezers, he slipped the blades of the scissors underneath the black one and around the red cable.

"Ten."

He snipped the red wire.

"It stopped." Tobias gave a deep exhale. "Five seconds left."

Henry grasped his knees and sucked in a breath. "The bomb has been neutralized."

"Yahoo!"

Chapter Sixteen

The SDPD bomb squad was in the process of securing the van full of explosives Henry had disarmed. The street had been evacuated of civilian personnel within at least fifty yards of the vehicle and police had cordoned off the area.

"Go ahead, Sandra," Tobias said, putting his phone on speaker for Henry to hear.

"There was a little less than half a pound of C-4 found in each of the three bombs," she said. "They were distractions, to test the loyalty of Vargas's men. Lansing helped protect Teflon's cover with a controlled detonation near Morley Elementary after the children had been evacuated. But we've got to cement it, sir. We need to make the other guy we have disappear. Pin all this on him as a snitch."

"Legally, we can hold him for fourteen days under the Patriot act without formal charges," Tobias said. "After that, things start to get tricky. It will have to be enough time for Teflon to finish building an ironclad case."

"Can't Teflon connect Vargas to the C-4?" Henry asked. "We can use that to arrest him."

"If his lawyers don't find a loophole and the charge

sticks," Tobias said, "which is a big *if* considering we don't have the driver of this van and possession of explosives is a *wobbler* here in California. It can be prosecuted as either a misdemeanor or a felony. Vargas has no criminal record. A misdemeanor is one year in county and/or a thousand-dollar fine. Depending on how long he's in custody awaiting trial, he might get time served. Felony charges would be two to three years and/or a ten-thousand-dollar fine. In the end, arresting him for this doesn't help you get Ben."

With a curse of frustration, Henry looked away. No matter what Vargas did, what line he crossed, he somehow managed to avoid getting caught.

"Sandra, cut Teflon loose," Tobias said. "We need Vargas on double-digit charges that will stick. Put the other guy in FBI custody quietly and get the word out among the first responders that a tip from an insider who's been long entrenched in *Los Chacales* saved the day."

Rather than spoon-feed that tidbit directly to the media, the information would spread like wildfire, taking on a life of its own. By the time it made its way to the press, the information would sound organic, not canned.

After Sandra acknowledged the order, Tobias disconnected and looked at Henry. "Come on. They're waiting on us."

Tobias led the way into the restaurant that had been targeted, to a private room where the marshals had apparently been having a going-away luncheon for Nick. Six marshals were standing by to talk to them.

Once the door was closed, Draper asked, "Does Allison need to be charged with conspiracy?"

A red-hot flash of indignation washed over Henry. "What in the hell are you talking about now?" He folded his arms, trying hard not to let anger cloud his head.

"Someone who knew we'd be here, like sitting ducks, told Vargas," Draper said. "Allison was aware of this luncheon. Maybe she made a deal. Us for your son."

Lowering his arms, Henry stepped forward as he clenched his fists, but Tobias flew in between them before Henry knocked Draper's lights out.

"You're a despicable man," Henry said. "That's the last time you accuse my wife of something she didn't do. She's got more honor in her pinkie toe than you do in your entire wretched body."

"Then how do you explain that van full of explosives parked outside?" Draper asked.

The other marshals looked back and forth at both men, taking everything in quietly.

Henry had given that some thought after the bomb squad had the situation under control. "The same way Vargas knew to contact us on a Minecraft forum. He sent Allison a phishing email. It looked like something from Ben's school and she clicked on a link. He's had remote access to her computer, probably sniffing around in her emails and documents for days. Any of your home computers could've been hacked, as well."

The marshals talked among themselves for a minute. It was clear on their faces they believed Henry.

"We'll have IT take a look at our personal computers," Draper said.

"That van outside is your fault." Henry pointed a finger at Draper. "If you had let Allison hold the press conference, instead of having her arrested on a bogus charge, Vargas never would've tried to blow you to kingdom come."

"Arrested?" Nick asked as the others murmured in shock.

"Of course you didn't bother to tell them," Henry said. "I guess you didn't want to spoil the farewell luncheon."

"We found Lynn Jacobs." Tobias stared at Draper. "Staying unavailable for a few hours is one thing. I doubt she'll lie under oath for you. Get on the phone with Captain Roessler and have Allison released from jail immediately. Or I'll keep my appointment with the deputy director of the US Marshals Service. He's expecting my call soon."

Draper gave a wry grin. "I spoke to the director before I met with you all earlier. He wasn't happy to be woken up, but he understood the urgency of the situation. I was authorized to suspend Allison for insubordination if she didn't back down."

Henry hid his surprise. "I'm sure you weren't authorized to have her arrested."

"The director is concerned about the damage Allison could do to the USMS by holding a rogue press conference. I was given the flexibility to take whatever course of action I deemed necessary to stop her. So, I did. I had her arrested to protect her."

A low, scornful laugh escaped Henry. "Give me a break." This guy was unbelievable. "You did that to protect yourself. Not Allison."

Draper sighed. "Once the press conference is off the table as an option, she's as good as free in my book. If Allison goes forward with it, you'll see the director on the news first. He'll start a smear campaign that will ruin her career."

Henry reeled back. "Smear her with what? She's one of the best marshals you have."

"She is." Draper nodded in agreement. "But do you know about the issues we had keeping our witness Lori Carpenter safe?"

Henry had only learned about it yesterday. "The one who was being protected up at Big Bear for a year."

"Nick was assigned." Draper gestured to him, and Nick gave a rueful nod. "He can attest to the hell they went through keeping her alive and getting her on the stand. We were even under physical attack at the USMS building."

Henry recalled the terror of wondering if Allison was okay when the news broke of the USMS being under siege. Of course, there hadn't been any mention in the media that it had been related to a witness preparing to testify, and Allison had neglected to share.

All he knew that day was he loved his wife and son more than anything and didn't want to lose them.

"It was another marshal who helped Vargas breach our database and compromised Lori's location," Draper said. "But the Department of Justice has investigated this, and they believe if Lori had never been up at Big Bear to begin with, then all those *issues* might've been avoided. I disagree, as does Nick."

"The only reason Lori and I survived is thanks to the terrain of Big Bear and the isolation," Nick said. "I shudder to think what would've happened if we had been at a safe house here in the city."

"Thus far," Draper said, "the director has held the wolves at bay, but Allison vetted Big Bear as the best location. I signed off on it." Draper raised his palm, emphasizing his admission. "But the director will make her the scapegoat to spare the agency any embarrassment in regard to a press conference. Once she's been discredited, no one in the media will take her seriously. Any admissions of remorse to the cartel on her part will be worthless. And her career..." Draper shook his head.

It would be over.

"I have great respect for Allison," Draper said, "and hold her in high esteem. I don't want her sitting in a jail cell. Assure me the PR nightmare of a press conference goes away and I will happily call Captain Roessler."

Henry considered the factors, weighing them. A press conference had always struck him as wrong anyway. Vargas knew the names of the US marshals in the San Diego office. He knew where they lived, who their spouses and children were. Heck, he'd proved it by sending vans with a half pound of C-4 to their schools. Odds were he'd also hacked their personal computers.

What was the point of having Allison stand up in front of the press?

To humiliate the marshals? To ruin her career?

Was this just sport for Vargas? What was his endgame?

Since they couldn't deliver Isabel today, they had to give him something of worth that he genuinely wanted to appease him. But they had to figure out what that was first, and Henry needed Ally to do that.

She might be upset with him for making this decision, but her sitting in jail wasn't helping anyone, least of all Ben.

"No press conference," Henry said. "You have my word. Now make the call."

"Consider it done." Draper got on his phone. "Hello, Captain Roessler," he said, walking out into the hall.

"I don't know if Special Agent Keogh told you, Henry," Nick said, "but I'm the liaison for the marshals on the kidnapping. Draper phased me out of everything else in the office since I'm getting ready to transfer and he thought I might be able to help. Until our invitation to the party was revoked. I'm not doing much of anything until I fly to Las Vegas. With the leadership concerned with what's best for the agency, we need to look out for each other. If you want me back, I'm at your disposal."

Henry had always liked Nick. A straight shooter, candid, sometimes a bit brusque, but he was no-nonsense and produced results. More important, he could be trusted.

"We could use the help," Henry said. "Consider your invite restored."

CAPTAIN ROESSLER UNLOCKED and opened the holding cell door with a smile. "You're free to go."

"What happened?" Allison didn't waste a second getting out of the bullpen.

"US Marshal Draper recanted. Turns out it was a misunderstanding," Roessler said. "Your husband is here, waiting for you, along with Special Agent Keogh. I'll walk you out." The captain led the way from holding, through the station. "You've missed quite a lot in lockup."

Ally had been in the holding cell less than five hours, but it had felt like a whole day. "Anything to do with my son?"

"Nothing on that front, sorry, but you should know your husband is a hero."

That meant Henry had done something that could've gotten him killed. "Please tell me he's all right." She braced herself to see him bandaged or wounded, but the important thing was that he was alive and waiting for her.

"He is. None the worse for wear."

The wave of relief that hit her highlighted her need to hear Henry's voice, to see his face.

They stopped at the plate-glass window of the personal property desk.

Roessler waved for the uniformed officer to hurry up as she signed on the clipboard. The captain took the manila envelope offered and handed it to her.

She opened the five-by-seven envelope and dumped the single item into her palm. Her wedding band. Once they'd decided to go to a hotel, it had felt weird to leave behind, even weirder to carry it in her pocket.

Allison slipped the eternity ring on her finger and fiddled with it. The day Henry had surprised her with the diamond band, she'd been so excited to put it on, but even more eager to marry him. Now, she wasn't sure if that life still fit her and the prospect of ever letting another man touch her was so foreign, it was preposterous.

"How did Henry save the day?" she wondered, and not for the first time since he'd joined HRT. "What happened?"

Asking Henry was pointless. He always downplayed everything. Not only because he was humble—another thing she loved about him—but also because he wouldn't want her worrying. Not about what he'd already survived, but about what he might face in the future on the job. He minimized the danger whenever he explained and she in turn had to get the cringeworthy specifics from Tobias.

"He disarmed a car bomb. Saved a lot of lives, including those of your fellow marshals. I heard from my guys that there was, like, two seconds left on the timer."

A cold blade of fear stabbed through her. *He's safe*, she had to remind herself.

Captain Roessler opened one of the double doors and escorted her to the front desk, where Henry and Tobias were standing.

Tempering the urge to run to Henry, she took him in for a moment instead. Wind-tossed hair. A bit too much color in that face of his that she always found hard to resist, as if his emotions were still running high, or perhaps it was the aftereffect of adrenaline. Dark scruff on his jaw that she longed to feel grazing her cheek.

Then those intense brown eyes met hers and a flutter in her belly replaced the fear.

They crossed the space of the lobby, meeting in the middle.

She put her palm to his chest, comforted beyond measure that he was okay. "I should've told you not to be a hero while I was behind bars."

"Sorry, but it couldn't be avoided."

Henry wasn't the type to sit back, playing it safe while others rushed into danger, no matter the sacrifice. No matter the personal toll on him or their family. It was just the way he was built. He practiced what he preached and set a stellar example for Ben by how he lived his life.

"I suppose not," she said. "Were there really only two seconds left on the timer?"

As if he could sense her muscles reflexively tightening, he pulled her into a hug. "No. There was loads of time left," he said, smooth and reassuring.

"Yeah," Tobias scoffed. "Try *five* seconds. We nearly died."

She could always count on Tobias for the unvarnished truth.

"That's still way too close for comfort in my book," Roessler said.

The thought of almost losing Henry, having to live in a world where he was gone, knocked the breath from her lungs. He was her first love, her only love. Even after living apart for months, it was impossible to picture a future without him.

Allison lifted on the balls of her feet and pressed her lips to Henry's cheek, to the deceptively soft brush of hair on his face. The kiss was quick, but her skin heated with awareness. "I'm glad you're all right."

He smiled down at her. The tender look warmed her heart. He took her other hand in his and gave it a squeeze like he'd never let her go.

Tobias's cell phone rang, and he excused himself.

"What did you do to get US Marshal Draper to recant?" Roessler asked.

"I was wondering myself," she said.

As Henry's smile fell, she knew she wasn't going to like the answer.

"I had to agree that you wouldn't give a press conference."

Roessler's eyebrows shot up and he stepped over to the front desk, wisely keeping whatever he was thinking to himself.

Allison pulled away from Henry, staring at him in

disbelief. "Why? How could you endanger Ben like that?"

"It's complicated. I didn't want to decide without you, but I had to get you out of jail. You should know that Draper has the support of the director of the US Marshals Service," he said, the announcement silencing her. "Trust me, a press conference would not have worked in our favor to get Ben back and it would've meant the end of your career."

"One minute, Chief," Tobias said on the phone, and hurried over to them. "I've got the chief of the Federal Ministerial Police in Mexico on the line."

Captain Roessler joined the huddle at the news.

"They got a hit on one of the photos we sent them. A driver's license for a Lourdes Suarez. They have an address and their agents are preparing to raid the place now." Tobias hit a button on the phone. "Chief Ocampo, you're on speaker. I have the parents here, Special Agent Boyd and Deputy Marshal Boyd, as well as police captain Roessler."

"We are outside her home, preparing to raid it."

"Chief, this is Special Agent Boyd. Why didn't you give us a heads-up that you had found the woman before organizing this raid?"

Allison understood Henry's concern. He had specialized training specifically for hostage rescue that far exceeded what any SWAT team on either side of the border had. They should've been consulted first before a team was prepped to go in hot.

"It was our understanding that this was time-sensitive, of the utmost urgency," Chief Ocampo said. "The less lead time that is given when acting against the cartel, the better our results."

That was code for they had leaks. Officers on the cartel's payroll. Tension coiled in Allison's stomach.

"There is a DEA agent stationed with one of our units who has agreed to come along, wearing his own body camera. I believe you have access to the system he uses, Omega Lookout. If so, you can watch along in real time."

"We also use that software here," Captain Roessler said, "but I'll need an authorization code."

"Let me know when you're ready to copy."

Roessler grabbed a pen and paper from the front desk. "Go ahead."

Chief Ocampo passed on the authorization code. "We're breaching the door in two minutes."

Chapter Seventeen

Captain Roessler led the way to his office. To keep pace with Roessler's ground-eating stride, Allison had to jog. Henry and Tobias were right behind her.

In his office, Roessler headed to his computer. He waved them to come around behind his desk and logged in. On the screen was an icon for Omega Lookout. The versatile law enforcement tool allowed command staff to see and hear what was happening as the situation unfolded. Roessler moved the mouse and clicked on it, but the app took a few seconds to load.

After he entered his username and password, he found the menu option to join a livestream and input the authorization code.

The live feed popped up in the app. Tapping the enlarge icon, Roessler brought the streaming video onto the entire screen. Then he backed away, letting them gather around in front.

The DEA agent on-site turned in a circle, giving them a three-hundred-sixty-degree view of the urban area. A black SUV and SWAT tactical truck were parked in front of a row of low-rise apartment buildings. The audio was crisp and clear. Police had blocked off the traffic from the street and waved passersby to get out of the way.

"Where exactly are they?" Henry asked.

"Culiacán," Tobias said.

That rang a bell in Allison's head. "Sinaloa?"

"Yes." Tobias nodded. "*Los Chacales* controls the region. It's the cartel's main hub in Mexico."

"But eighteen, nineteen hours from here." Henry shook his head as if something were off. "Not even on the outer fringe of Culiacán. The heart of a large metropolitan area doesn't make sense."

"Why?" Allison asked.

"I have to get you up to speed on a few things. After the raid."

She nodded, refocusing her full attention on the monitor.

SWAT officers were dressed in tactical gear, their faces covered, helmets, protective eyewear, assault rifles at the ready. A six-man squad moved across the parking lot, carrying a battering ram. They hurried inside the small, three-story building and swept up the stairs to the second floor. The assault team scurried to both sides of a doorway, pressing their backs to the wall.

Two officers rushed the door with the large ram. With one swift hit, the door flew open and the two-man team hustled backward out of the way.

Someone lobbed a flash-bang inside. The grenade went off. A burst of blinding white light and a deafening boom followed. The two million lumens and one hundred eighty decibels would incapacitate anybody in the front rooms of the apartment. Including her son.

He was only seven. The light, the sound, would be utterly terrifying for him.

Allison pressed her fingers to her mouth, swallowing back a thick lump of fear. Her heart slammed against her rib cage.

The rest of the unit swarmed inside. Footsteps pounding through the apartment drove her heart to drum faster. Scanning the screen, she searched for Ben. Allison held her breath, dreading what the SWAT team might find and hoping at the same time, as they cleared room-to-room.

The kitchen, living room, one barren bedroom—not even a mattress—the closet, bathroom. There was nothing.

No one.

No sign of Ben anywhere.

"All clear!" someone called out. "The apartment is empty."

"No," Ally gasped. A deep ache seeped through her as if her entire body was one big bruise.

Henry wrapped his arm around her, pulling her against his side.

"Do you think they were tipped off?" she asked. "Maybe someone gave them a heads-up the police were on the way." Despair was beating her down to rock bottom.

One of the officers found a small bag in the closet. He unzipped it and dumped the contents, going through it. Men's clothes, two loaded magazines, a 9 mm and five hundred thousand pesos. Twenty grand in US dollars. A go bag for a criminal.

"If anyone had just left, they would've taken the bag," Tobias said, echoing her thoughts.

"Call Chief Ocampo back," Henry said.

Without hesitation, Tobias took out his cell and dialed. A minute later the chief was on speakerphone.

"This is Special Agent Boyd again. Chief, is there a wind turbine anywhere close by."

"Wind turbine?" the chief asked, sounding as confused as Allison was. "No. We're in the city. There are no turbines."

"Can you ask the DEA agent to check the refrigerator?" Henry asked.

The request went out over the chief's radio. The DEA agent flew into motion in response, making his way to the kitchen.

He opened the fridge. The shelves were bare.

"Thank you, Chief Ocampo."

"I'm sorry we didn't find your son. If we turn up anything else, we'll let you know."

Tobias took the phone, thanking the chief again for their responsiveness and assistance.

"They were never there," Henry said to Allison, putting a supportive hand on her shoulder.

"What do you mean?"

"Ben was never in that apartment." He gripped her tighter as if to communicate *stay strong*. "I doubt he's in Culiacán at all. He may not even be in Mexico. It's possible he's still here in California."

"How can you be so sure?"

"I haven't had a chance to tell you. We received proof of life. A video of Ben taken this morning."

Her heart clutched with desperation to see it.

"WHAT'S WRONG?" Lourdes followed her brother to the window. The look on his face was enough to make her stomach convulse, threatening to bring her lunch up.

Javier stared at his phone. "It's my crash pad in Culiacán. First, someone activated the trip wire. Now this." He showed her the text message.

Americans looking for you and a boy. They have your sister's name.

Her brother paid the police in Culiacán as well as Ensenada for information, and to turn a blind eye when necessary.

"Do we need to leave?" she asked.

"You tell me." He fixed her with a pointed stare. "Does Principal Garcia know this address?"

"No." Lourdes shook her head emphatically. "She asked once, telling me that the PO box in the city wasn't sufficient. Then you made the big donation and kept making them every year. She dropped it."

"Is your photo on file at the school?"

"It was optional for everyone, but I passed. I've been careful. The way you taught me."

To stay with her brother meant living by his rules. She even used her mother's maiden name at the school, blaming it on an ex who harassed her. No one questioned it. She was friendly with everyone at work, but she kept her distance and didn't have any friends there. No one to pry into her business.

He cupped her jaw, put his forehead to hers, and the concern in his face lifted. "I don't want to risk changing locations if we don't have to. Additional exposure would be bad." Letting her go, he glanced at Ben. "The kid likes the video games. I want him to play upstairs in the guest room. I'll set up a TV and move the game console."

"Why?" she whispered. "He likes it down here."

"I need to tighten up control of the environment."

He was still worried and was trying to hide it. She could tell. "Are you sure everything is okay?"

"Yeah. I just need to be vigilant."

WATCHING ALLY STARE at the photo with glassy eyes pained Henry. The timing of when the video had been sent was pure bad luck. An hour earlier, heck, thirty minutes, and she could've seen it before it had been erased.

But Vargas had remotely deleted the video, robbing her of the chance to see their son was unharmed and to hear his voice.

It was so unfair that she'd been cheated.

He tore his gaze from the rearview mirror in the car and looked back at the road.

"We're going to get a break," Tobias said. "Soon. You'll see."

They had to believe that and hold on to it.

"Ally," Henry said, turning into the hotel's garage. "You should know the team has set up in the adjoining room."

She murmured something, but he caught her head nod in acknowledgment as he parked.

Everyone filed out of the car and got into the elevator.

Henry stretched his neck from side to side and rolled his shoulders, knowing he had to prep Allison before she saw Sandra. She didn't deserve to be blindsided. "About the team upstairs…" Henry started, not quite sure if it might be better to talk in private.

"I've got the best working this," Tobias said, his voice

booming with confidence. "Rosalind, CJ and Sandra. And, uh, Nick McKenna should be up there by now, too."

Ally gave another slow head nod. "Okay. Sounds good," she said numbly.

Henry and Tobias exchanged a glance in the reflection of the elevator doors. Allison stared straight ahead, as if she wasn't really looking at anything at all.

The elevator chimed and the doors opened. They made their way down the hall. Henry followed Tobias and Allison into the makeshift command center.

The room was abuzz with activity.

"Is Teflon good to go?" Tobias asked.

"He should be," Sandra said. "Part of *Los Chacales*' protocol is for him to take his time going back, to make sure no one saw him and that he wasn't followed. The other guy is sitting in holding. Dawes will take care of him."

Nick came over to Ally. "How are you holding up?"

"I guess as well as can be expected." She shrugged. "I'm glad you're here."

"Happy to be of service, especially after what Draper did to you," Nick said with a look of disgust. "Anything you need, let me know."

"Actually, there might be something you can do." Allison pulled him to the side and motioned for Henry to join them. "Are you up to speed on everything? How we've failed to deliver on all the demands?"

"Yeah," Nick said. "How can I help?"

"When Vargas contacts us again, we need to give him something. I want to give him Lori."

What the hell?

"You can't be serious." Nick scowled at the idea. "I'm not letting that monster anywhere near my fiancée."

"Not her, physically. I mean her location in Phoenix. When is she flying out to Las Vegas? Do you think you can get her on a flight today?"

"She's already there, settling in with my family until we can look for a place together."

"That's perfect." Allison's eyes brightened. "The press conference is off the table, I know, and I think I can get Vargas to drop the issue—in exchange for Lori. He must want her more than the other witnesses."

Nick's mouth flattened. "Because they were once involved."

Allison nodded. "I want to give him her Phoenix address and the new name the USMS gave her."

"That could be tricky, hon," Henry said. "A marriage license is a matter of public record. Once Nick and Lori get one, Vargas could track her down."

"Not if they got married here. California is the only state that allows a couple to get a confidential marriage license."

"What about when she gets a job?" Henry asked.

"That won't be a problem," Nick said. "She's going to work for my family. We can keep her off the books until after we're married."

Allison flashed a hopeful smile. "Then it's possible."

"It is," Nick said. "Let me call Lori and run it by her. I'm sure she'll agree to anything to get your son back, but you know how it is."

Henry sighed. "I do." And he was still learning.

"Allison, Henry." Rosalind called them to CJ's workstation. "You're going to want to see this."

"Thank you," Ally said to Nick before they went to see what Rosalind had found.

"I combed through all the surveillance feeds within

a five-block radius of your house and found nothing, the same as the police. But then I checked to see if there were any speeding cameras at other points within that radius, and there are. Every vehicle that passes one gets recorded, even if it wasn't speeding. I found the van," Rosalind said with cocky smile.

"More important," CJ said, "with those particular cameras, you can zoom in." CJ hit a few buttons and brought up an image of the windshield of the black van. The same man who had chased Ben in the park was behind the wheel. *El Escorpion.* "We got the VIN number."

Tobias and Sandra came over, listening in.

"Great. But how does that help us find Ben?" Allison asked, stepping around the back of CJ's chair to the other side, moving away from Sandra.

The action was subtle, but it was hard for Henry not to notice.

"By itself, it doesn't," CJ said.

"But I scrutinized the surveillance from the park." Rosalind put her hands on her hips. "After they grabbed Ben again, it was safe to assume they hightailed it out of there as quickly as possible. The police were right. No black van was in the area."

CJ clacked on the keyboard, hit Enter and brought up another photo. "The van is now white."

"The same van?" Henry asked.

A finger click away was the answer as another photo came onto the screen. The picture was of the front of the white van. The same man driving. Then CJ zoomed in. The same VIN number, as well.

"Oh, God," Ally said. "They changed the van color."

"And the plates," CJ said.

Rosalind nodded. "That's why the cops couldn't find them, but we were able to track it from the park."

Ally looked as hopeful as Henry felt, but Rosalind's smile fell. Whatever she was going to say next wasn't good news.

"We traced it all the way to the border before we lost them," Rosalind said. "They're somewhere in Mexico."

"No, no, no." Allison shook her head. "They just searched for them in Culiacán and they weren't there."

"Culiacán is too far," Henry said. "In the video, the kidnapper mentioned cooking Ben dinner. That means they were someplace where he had access to a kitchen last night. Maybe an eight- to ten-hour drive max from San Diego. Not eighteen, nineteen hours to Culiacán."

Allison drew a deep breath, visibly calming. "How do we find them?"

Henry's thoughts sharpened in focus and he snapped his fingers. "The wind turbine."

"I'm already working that angle." CJ rolled down to the next monitor. A few clicks and a map of the Baja California Peninsula in Mexico came up. "All the red dots are wind farms."

There were twelve dots scattered across the peninsula.

"Good grief," Allison muttered.

"Only show us the ones within a ten-hour drive," Henry said.

CJ made quick work of filtering the wind farms, reducing the number to six.

"How do we search all those?" Allison asked.

"Let me see what I can do," Tobias said. "ICE has UAVs to help with border patrol. I can see about requisitioning one. But it could take a couple of hours to get an answer one way or the other."

"What are we supposed to do in the meantime?" Allison asked. "Twiddle our thumbs and wait for Vargas to call?"

"When was the last time either of you slept, huh?" Tobias meant it as a rhetorical question because he didn't wait for a response. "Go get some rest. We survived the afternoon *and* we've made progress. That's a lot. Take comfort in it and recharge."

Tobias was right. If they kept going like this, they'd burn out. Have nothing left in the tank when they needed it most.

Thankfully, Allison nodded, not fighting the advice.

"If we have any urgent updates, we'll call, and if Vargas contacts you again, be sure to let us know."

"Will do," Henry said. "Thank you, everyone. We appreciate it." He traipsed behind Allison into their own room and shut the door that connected it to the adjoining space.

She headed into the bedroom. Kicking off her shoes, Allison pulled the elastic band from around her ponytail, freeing her black, glossy hair to fall around her shoulders.

God, he loved her hair. Her soft skin. Her smile.

Her everything.

"Hey." Henry caught Allison by the arm. "Hon, if you need Sandra to leave, just say the word."

Allison glanced up at him and their eyes locked. "And how would that look?"

"Who cares how it looks? Tobias can pull someone from HRT to help."

"Then why didn't he?"

The others on HRT, with the exception of Valentine, were resting up in case they found Ben and were needed to go in. It was bad enough Henry was exhausted. They didn't need fatigue messing with any other members on the small team.

When he didn't immediately respond, she said, "Exactly." She was all too familiar with the drill and their protocol.

"We've got Nick in there to cover down. He's smart and capable."

"Can we be honest with each other? No walking on eggshells?"

Since Ben was taken, they'd both been brutally honest. Talking like two people with nothing to lose and nothing to gain besides closure. Perhaps they should've tried that a year ago.

"Absolutely," he said, his throat tight and his sense of forbearance worn threadbare.

"Do you want to be with Sandra? Did you ever *want* her? Even a little."

Henry blinked at her, the questions blindsiding him. But he had nothing to hide. Not from Ally.

Chapter Eighteen

Allison wanted all their cards on the table. No secrets. No lies. No omissions.

She believed nothing had happened while they were together. Who was to know if he and Sandra had tested the waters once he'd moved out? He would've had every right after she'd asked him to leave. She simply wanted to know.

With the world unraveling and the ground like quicksand beneath her feet, she needed one thing to be solid and true. Her relationship with Henry. Whether as spouses or co-parents, she had to be able to count on him to be honest. Even if the truth hurt.

"Never," Henry said with such conviction she felt it in her heart. "I swear on my life, I've never had any interest in her." He cupped her shoulders and held her gaze.

"Then I have to take you at your word," she said softly. "I don't want to fight with you anymore." She didn't have the strength to go on the attack or to play defense. "I don't have enough left in reserve for it. Especially not to stress out about Sandra. There are more important issues."

Sandra was nothing more than a footnote in their

lives, but that didn't mean Allison had to stand next to her, inhaling her obnoxious perfume.

She was pleased he'd offered to get rid of her, but Allison wasn't petty and far from delusional. They needed as much help, as many pairs of eyes and hands, on this as possible.

Nothing was going to stand in the way of her getting Ben back. Least of all the green-eyed monster. She'd gone up against bigger demons and prevailed.

"I'm so sorry I pushed you away with my actions," Henry said, his gaze burning into hers. "That I made you feel alone. Hurt you. Made you doubt me."

She knew he was sorry and that if he had it to do over again, his choices would've been different. But it wasn't all his fault. "I'm sorry I shut you out instead of fighting…for us." It had been so hard when she was caught up in the middle of things to think straight, to see clearly.

He rubbed up and down her arms and caressed her shoulders. "I have a confession. When we separated, I've never been so lonely in my life. It wasn't because I was alone. It was because I wasn't with you. Since we've been together, I have never been tempted to stray."

His unsolicited admission left her speechless, held her rooted in place. A decade was a long time to be with someone. Longer still not to have been tempted by another.

Time hadn't diminished her attraction to Henry, but a part of her thought it might have been different for him. She was relieved that it hadn't been. Reassured. Flattered.

He raised a hand and stroked her cheek with his

knuckles. A tender caress that had slow-burning awareness spilling down her spine.

It would have been a fleeting moment if she had
moved away from his touch, but she didn't.

Life was so short. She'd wasted a year being angry,
holding on to the hurt, when she could have lost him
today. Five seconds on the timer.

Five.

"It's always been you, Ally," he said in a husky tone,
his voice thick with emotion. "Always, only you." He
lowered his head to hers. "I love you," he whispered
against her lips.

The next thing she knew, she was in his arms, as if
gravity had pulled her there. His hand dove into her
hair, cupping the nape of her neck and bringing her
mouth to his.

Emotions surged in a strange mixture of tenderness
and necessity.

His lips were firm and demanding, sweeping over
hers. She closed her eyes and opened to him. One soul
reaching out to another. Both clamoring for consolation,
for something warm and safe to hold on to.

They breathed each other in, hurting like hell, and
needing to feel something good. Light breaking through
the darkness, for a little while.

As his fingers threaded through her hair, he deepened the kiss. Her nerve endings tingled to life. Her skin
awake and itching for his hands, exploring, pursuing.

Their jackets and shirts flew off in the dim light
of the drawn curtains. He unhooked her bra, letting it
fall to the floor, and she unfastened his belt, pulling it
from his pants.

Sliding her arms around his neck, she drank him in.

The feel of him hard and solid against her front sent a bolt of exhilaration through her.

Something sweet and irresistible spread to her extremities, tickling her fingers and toes.

She trusted him with her body and hated how she'd feared with her heart. But she wanted to push past the pain, give in to the bittersweet ache.

Longing twisted deep inside her, tightening in her veins and stealing her breath. A desire so strong she didn't want to resist it.

Her body bowed, aching to get as close as possible, desperate for friction. Henry must've felt the same urgency, lifting her up with one hand on her bottom and the other locked on her thigh. She leaned against the window. Shuddered at the way they slid against each other, finding a natural rhythm.

His eyes were almost black with naked yearning. Her hand was buried in the thick waves of his hair as her legs scrambled for purchase.

She gripped his arm tighter, trying to hold herself up as he weakened her with every caress, each blistering kiss. His muscles flexed under her palm. Not the big, bulky kind. Henry's body was lean and sinewy and strong. Sexy.

Instead of hastily taking his pleasure, he lowered to his knees, dragging her slacks and underwear down with him, and gave it slowly.

Heat fluttered low and hot. Her thoughts evaporated the second he kissed her *there*. Made love to her with his tongue, soothed the pain he'd brought her, showered her with affection using his clever fingers that found her wet and wanting. Needing him, craving skin on skin everywhere.

Oh, God, she thought, the truth striking her like a bolt of lightning. Henry Boyd had ruined her for other men. The one year of abstinence only intensified her longing, coiled tight through her until she was ready to snap. Her release came hard and fast, tearing through her.

Then her legs buckled, but Henry caught her and carried her to the bed. After he laid her down gently, he stripped off the rest of his clothes and dropped down beside her. Played in her hair, ran his nose along the shell of her ear, and she remembered what it felt like, the splendor of belonging to each other. This cocoon where time stopped and the world faded to dust.

Running her gaze over his bare skin, her belly flip-flopped, but without giving doubt a chance to bulldoze through their moment, she moved over him. Still throbbing, she trailed kisses down his belly while stroking him with her hand and then took him into her mouth.

Groaning, he submitted to her control. She felt his muscles loosening as he gave in to the comfort of physical connection.

"Stop," he gasped. "Please."

She eased off him, only enough to straddle his hips and guide him home. Her heartbeat seemed to have migrated to the apex of her thighs. The pleasure was overwhelming. Too much. But it was nothing compared to the sharp-edged sense of communion. The feeling of being with him *was* like coming home, to that nurturing place where she fit perfectly with another. She missed this intimacy when it had stopped, in a way that she craved.

Her body zeroed in on that point of friction, on the

hot rush of need, her hips driving him. And hunger consumed them, taking them both over the edge.

Sated and spent, hearts beating wildly, they curled up together.

For a long moment, they stayed like that. His body pressed to hers, his hand in her hair, his scent wrapping around her.

He smoothed his fingers over her hair, brushed his lips across her forehead, pulling on a thousand threads of memory. Of falling in love with him. Of how good they'd been as a couple, a family. The way they'd brought out the best in each other. Birthdays, holidays, anniversaries they'd shared. To all the days and nights that they were still supposed to have together.

She was so tangled up in Henry, she couldn't see a future without him. They were bound by history, by love, pain, fear...Ben. One common goal.

He trembled, or she had first, unable to tell because they were so close, their bodies as one. Allison laid her head against his shoulder and drew him tighter. Locked in an embrace that she didn't want to end.

"I love you so much it hurts," he said, his voice a harsh whisper. "I don't ever want to be apart from you."

Her breath snagged in her throat, her heart chasing after it. She leaned up on her forearm and stared down at him. "What are you saying? You—you still want us?"

"Yes." His answer was raw and certain. The same as the look on his face.

"But you signed the divorce papers." He'd agreed to everything when she'd thought they'd have more time to sort out their feelings.

"Because that's what you wanted. I never wanted to leave our bed, our house, you or Ben. I only did it because you asked it of me. I've always wanted us. Always will. Being without you is like living half a life. I want our family."

What was she supposed to say to that?

She felt the same, but was it real? Were their emotions fuzzy and unreliable because they'd made love?

Sex didn't magically solve problems; though, in the afterglow, it seemed as such.

Then the cell phone rang and everything between them shifted to the back burner.

Henry answered his phone, putting it on speaker. "We're both here."

"I spoke with the deputy secretary of the Department of Homeland Security," Tobias said. "He conferred with the commissioner of Customs and Border Protection. They won't re-task their Predator drones to help us."

Ally's heart sank, but Henry squeezed her hand, a sign not to give up hope.

"Can you take it higher? Go above their heads?" Henry asked.

"That would take time we don't have, but they did propose a solution. They're testing new, cheaper, smaller drones that they're willing to let us use. The speed and flight time aren't quite the same. It'll take longer to cover the same area, but we'll have three.

"Rosalind and Sandra are heading down to the CBP surveillance hub near the border to oversee things. CJ thinks starting with the farms in Tecate and Mexicali is the best strategy. We'll look for houses near a wind turbine based on CJ's calculations from the photo. We'll also search for the van. If nothing turns up there, we'll move south."

"Thank you," Ally said.

"No problem. Sorry to disturb, but I thought you'd feel better knowing the search is moving forward."

"We appreciate the call. If there's anything else, don't hesitate to let us know."

After Tobias agreed, he put Nick on. "Hey, Lori is cool with you giving up her information if it'll buy you some time. She knows what kind of monster you're up against and she's safe with my family. They won't let anything happen to her."

Allison exhaled in relief. "You and Lori are the best. Thanks so much, Nick."

Henry expressed his thanks and hung up. He pulled her against him in a hug. "We're going to find him. Soon. We'll bring Ben home. Alive and unharmed."

She tightened her arms around him and prayed he was right.

IN THE LUSH COURTYARD, Emilio sat and waited, staring out at the ocean. He sipped his Scotch. A thirty-year-old Isle of Jura. The flavors rolled on his tongue—fresh grain, orange peel and toffee—and the smooth, rich heat slid down his throat.

Lucas and Samuel had returned unscathed. Both vans had been parked at the specified locations, but the bombs hadn't detonated. The explosives meant for the marshals had come close, down to the wire.

But only one bomb had gone off. At Morley Field.

Scrutinized by itself, it meant nothing and could have been orchestrated, but if the driver also returned, then he'd know which man could be trusted. And who had betrayed him.

It was all over the news about an anonymous tip that had subverted Emilio's plan. Word on the street was that the mole in his operation had returned to the FBI fold, fearing his cover had been blown while trying to protect the children at the schools.

But Emilio struggled to believe it. Not until he saw who returned with his own eyes.

"He's back," Lucas said behind him.

The two words echoed in Emilio's head like a death knell. With dread and anticipation, he swiveled in his chair and looked over his shoulder.

Max strode down the walkway toward him, a confident smile on his face. "Mission accomplished, though I was shocked the yield had been so low."

Emilio didn't know whether to curse in disappointment that he'd lost Rodrigo or cheer in victory for having smoked out his rat.

His top lieutenant had betrayed him. *Rodrigo.* Did the FBI have something on him? Or was he still bitter that Emilio hadn't left him in charge in Sinaloa?

Refocusing on Max, Emilio said, "You stuck around to watch the bomb detonate?"

"Yeah. I watched from a distance to make sure it went off as expected. You said this was important." Max looked around at Samuel and Lucas. "Where's Rodrigo?"

"He's not coming back," Emilio said with a heavy heart and at the same time utter relief. "He was an FBI informant. A despicable snake." He tossed back the Scotch in his glass.

"Rodrigo?" Max reeled in surprise. "No, I can't believe it. But then again…" His voice trailed off.

Emilio sat up and stared at him. "What? Tell me."

"Earlier when you told us not to share the information in our envelopes, I thought it was odd that Rodrigo flagged me down on the road and made me pull over."

"What for?" Emilio asked, rising from his chair.

"He wanted to know the location of my target."

Pinching his eyes closed, Emilio willed away the sting in his chest. "Did you tell him?"

"I gave him the name of another school, but not the one in my envelope. I picked Gold Heights at random. It was the only one I could think of."

That would explain the fire trucks at so many of the schools and how they'd found Lucas's van. But it still left Emilio wondering how they'd discovered and disarmed Samuel's bomb.

Maybe Max was the only one he could rely on for results. To follow orders without question. To be loyal and at his side to the end. Max had been leery of Dutch Haas from the moment he'd laid eyes on him and had warned Emilio repeatedly about trusting him.

Emilio dismissed Lucas and Samuel with a wave of his hand. He gestured for Max to sit and poured them both a Scotch.

"That's why you tested us," Max said, sniffing the Scotch. "I wish I had known sooner about a spy in our ranks. It's lucky you didn't tell him anything about the kidnapped boy."

Leaning forward and resting his forearms on the table, Emilio considered Max a moment. Of course, his men instinctively knew that he was responsible for the boy's abduction, but until he had weeded out the traitor, he could say nothing.

Luck had nothing to do with it.

"Yes, a good calculation on my part."

"What's the plan? Kill the kid or are you trying to barter him for something?"

"I want Isabel back."

Max's brow furrowed. "But even if she came back, she wouldn't stay. Why risk taking a marshal's kid?"

"They ripped her out of my life like a pack of wild animals. There's so much left unsaid between us. I never got the chance to say goodbye."

Max nodded, his eyes sympathetic, as if he understood. "Have you been in contact with the marshal?"

"I've been careful. Don't worry."

"Don't call her back. It's not safe. Let me post a couple of guys at the airport. If they are working on getting her to meet the demand, the odds are she'll fly in from somewhere. We intercept and cut out the middle man. That way this ends on your terms. Not theirs."

Emilio smiled and took a swallow of his Scotch. "I like the way you think. It's a good plan."

"The more interaction you have with them, the more opportunities you give them to lay a trap. Dangle some bait that you might be tempted to take."

"Yes. Very good." Emilio drained his glass and poured another two fingers. "All I truly want is Isabel and to make that marshal suffer." He had hoped to toy with the marshal a bit more, see if she'd reached rock bottom yet. But he was confident she was in hell right now, fretting over her son.

"Speaking of the kid," Max said. "I'm sure they're scouring the city looking for him. Let me check out the safe house where he's being kept. I'll make certain the site doesn't have any vulnerabilities that can be exploited. Lock it down tight."

"That won't be necessary." Emilio waved his hand.

"The boy isn't here in San Diego. He's in Mexico with *El Escorpion*."

Max paled. Everyone knew *El Escorpion*'s reputation. "In Culiacán?"

Emilio narrowed his eyes and studied Max's face. "No, not Culiacán. Why so many questions?"

For the briefest moment, he considered the odds of the FBI turning two informants at the highest level right under his nose. One must've been difficult. Two impossible.

And Max was taking precautionary steps to insulate him, put distance between him and the FBI. An informant would have encouraged further contact in the hope Emilio would slip up and make a mistake.

"It's my job to protect you and, with Rodrigo not here, I've got to do the work of two men. I'm just trying to look out for you, Don Emilio, and that means ensuring the marshals don't find that kid until *you're* ready."

Relief seeped through Emilio at Max's loyalty. This lieutenant would lay down his life for him. Emilio trusted him. To an extent. "Focus on intercepting Isabel at the airport. No more questions about the boy. You don't need to know where he is to keep me safe. *El Escorpion* has everything under control regarding the kid."

If the marshals found the child—tried to take Emilio's sole leverage—then Javier would do as Emilio had instructed.

Kill the boy and order the hit on the other target. But only as a last resort.

Chapter Nineteen

Three hours of sleep, a hot shower and a decent meal had done wonders for Henry and, he suspected, for Ally, too. But it was nothing compared to CJ's news.

"We got something," CJ said. "An FRS match."

"What's that?" Allison asked.

Henry put his hand on her shoulder. "A hit on facial recognition software."

"We'd only been running the program here in the San Diego area and outskirts. Once we confirmed that *El Escorpion* had crossed the border, I reset the program to cull through data in Mexico, restricting it to the range of a ten-hour drive."

"That's still a mountain of data," Nick added.

"But we got one hit on Lourdes Suarez." CJ clacked away and brought it up on the screen.

They stared at a picture posted on the Facebook page of an elementary school. She wasn't posing in the photo and had been caught in the background. If her head had been turned forty-five degrees away from the camera when it had been taken, they wouldn't be staring at her now.

"There's no Lourdes Suarez listed as a teacher," CJ

said. "But there is a Lourdes Marin. No picture of her on their website. This was the only thing I could find."

"Where's the school?" Henry asked.

"Ensenada." CJ brought up a map. "It's less than a three-hour drive from here, but there's no wind farm near that city."

"What if it's not a farm?" Henry wondered out loud. "What if it's a single turbine to power a house?"

CJ nodded. "It's possible. Wind technology is developing rapidly, especially for residential applications. Since she's a teacher at the school, what's a realistic commute time?"

"Thirty minutes," Allison said, "but it could be as long as an hour and a half if she's paranoid and has something to hide."

"How long to re-task the drones to search the city and outskirts?" Henry asked.

"Already done," Tobias said. "The drones are en route. I'll relay to Rosalind and Sandra that we might be looking for a single wind turbine instead of a farm."

"Do I have to wait for solid confirmation?" Henry asked. "Or can you green-light me now?"

"Get HRT prepped and ready. CJ will get you patched into the drone feed. Once we have confirmation, you are cleared for wheels up."

"Let us get in the air sooner rather than later," Henry protested, not wanting to waste precious time.

"If Ben is somewhere near Ensenada, then you can be there within thirty to forty-five minutes." Tobias patted his shoulder. "You need to know what you're walking into before you take off. I understand you're anxious and raring to go, but we'll do this by the book. Or I have to pull you from the team."

Henry had trained for this. Lived and breathed the job, knew protocol inside out. But when it came to Ben… This mission wouldn't succeed if he led it with out-of-check emotions. Hell, they might not be able to pull it off if he was leading. As head of his hostage rescue team, he'd consider benching one of his own if their kid were on the line.

Emotion clouded judgment. It was the simple, plain truth, and Henry was human. Fallible regardless of his years of experience. One bad call on his part and not only could a teammate end up dead, but also so could Ben.

He wanted to believe that he could find enough detachment to do the job with laser focus, but he wasn't one hundred percent confident.

"We'll wait until you give the go-ahead. If you choose to yank me as team lead," he said, hating the words, but needing to voice it, "I'll like it about as much as swallowing broken glass, but I'll accept your decision."

"Henry, since the moment we learned Ben was taken, do you think I've asked myself what role I was going to let you play if we came down to a hostage rescue situation?" Tobias said. "You have consistently demonstrated good judgment, including offering to step aside. You've got a small team. You'll need every man, and I wouldn't dream of messing with your synergy. I think it might cause more harm than good asking you take orders in-field from one of your guys. You're the best at this. I know you can handle it."

Tobias's reassurance meant the world to him. Gave him the boost of conviction that he needed.

"Thank you," Henry said. "I needed to hear that. I'll get the team prepped and the chopper ready to fly." He took Ally off to the side. "Tobias will keep you posted on everything."

"I know." She pressed her palms to his chest. "Be careful out there."

"Always."

"Henry, I don't know what's supposed to happen next between us. Sex has never been our issue, but it doesn't solve anything."

"You're right," he said with a nod. "We argue about something, then make love, and I tend to act like it's water under the bridge. When many times it's not. It takes hard work and honesty. I get it and I'm willing to give both."

She still looked hesitant. "One thing I know for certain is that I love you."

"Enough to go to counseling with me?"

Her eyes widened. "But you refused before."

"I was an idiot. I'll do whatever it takes to keep my family."

She brushed her cool fingers across his forehead. "Don't think about any of that right now. Do what you normally do before you go into the field. Block me and our problems out." She gave a soft chuckle. "Focus on the mission. Bring our baby home."

THE WAITING WAS the worst part for Allison. Two hours into the redirected search of Ensenada and the surrounding area was torture.

CJ had patched into the CBP surveillance center and received drone-relay snapshots, plotting out their digital progress on the map. The drones seemed to sputter through the sky, inching across the miles, when she needed them to soar.

The drones had twelve hours of gas, onboard sensors, a thermal imaging camera and near silent motors. Unlike the roar of the rotors on an incoming helicopter.

Henry and his team would have a tough job. The chopper would announce their presence and his team had to move swiftly and decisively. As they did each and every time they jumped into the fray.

From the pictures she'd seen, the resolution was top of the line. The Predator drone would've been preferred for speed and efficiency, but they had three of the smaller ones to scout the area.

Once they reached Ensenada, only one had been sent into the city to do a precautionary sweep. The other two drones had been sent out into the countryside.

The sun was setting, but the thermal camera would still be able to pick up a wind turbine from a distance.

Tobias's phone rang. He answered, talking out of earshot for a minute then hustling over to her where she stood next to Nick. "It's Sandra. You're going to want to hear this. Go ahead, Sandra, you're on speaker."

"I received a brief message from Teflon. Vargas admitted to the kidnapping. With Teflon's testimony, we'll have enough to put Vargas away. If we find Ben in Mexico, across the state line, it's a federal offense. Twenty years to life. You need to get a warrant."

"But we can't move against him until Henry gets Ben," Allison said, terrified of them taking a premature action that could end with Vargas giving the order to hurt her son.

"We can start on the process to get a warrant," Tobias said. "We'll go through a discreet judge we trust. That way, once Henry has Ben, we'll be ready to move on Vargas and charge him."

She thought about it for a moment. Nobody wanted Vargas behind bars more than she did. "Okay."

Tobias dove in, making phone calls, getting the wheels of justice turning while the rest of them looked over the drone relays.

Nick handed her a cup of coffee and she accepted it.

Tension and silence were heavy in the room. CJ sent the images from the two drones in the countryside to the monitor on the far right.

Allison strained to see the details in each snapshot as they came in. One after another. For a solid hour of scanning numerous photos, there was little more than gray splotches and darkness.

Finally, drone Bravo captured the image of a single wind turbine located near a house, miles from anything else.

That's it. In her gut, she knew it was the house they were looking for.

"No white van," Allison said, staring at a black SUV parked beside the two-story house in front of the detached two-car garage.

"Doesn't mean it's not there, parked in the garage. Rosalind, get the license plate," CJ said over the open line.

"We're on it and switching to livestream video."

The video record time was limited on the smaller drones as opposed to the Predator, which had a greater capacity. They had to use livestream when and where it counted most.

Dropping low behind the SUV, the drone poised in front of the license plate.

Immediately, CJ launched into action on the computer.

"What are you doing?" Nick asked.

"I hacked into the DMV in Baja and Sonora, looking to see who the van was registered to. Turned up stolen. I still have access." As he typed, he said, "Can we check out the inside of the detached garage through the windows? See if there are any vehicles inside."

"Will do," Rosalind said.

"The SUV is registered to a Javier Suarez. What do you want to bet that he's related to a Lourdes?" CJ looked at Allison with a smile.

The drone rose in the air, gliding to a window in the garage. There was a white van.

"The license plate is different," Allison said, noticing immediately.

"Doesn't mean anything." CJ looked at her. "He could've changed the plates again. Someone dumped your nanny's body near the police station. If was it him, using the same vehicle, it would make sense to change the plates again."

He was right. It made sense.

The drone's camera zoomed in on the windshield. They were in luck that the driver had backed in.

CJ read the VIN out loud, comparing it to the one on *El Escorpion*'s van. "We have a match on the vehicle. One hundred percent."

Tobias bent over next to CJ, near his phone that was on speaker. "Rosalind, check the house for signs of activity, but don't get too close to the windows."

"Roger, sir."

The drone circled the house, using the thermal-imaging sensor. Allison sipped her coffee to give herself something to do as she waited for anything to appear on the screen.

She was sick with worry. What if Ben wasn't there? What if he had been dropped off at an alternate location?

Fuzzy red blobs appeared on the second floor. Three heat signatures indicating people in one room. The thermal camera detected more than just heat, picking up the differences between heat sources. It looked like a television was on, giving off electromagnetic energy. Two people sat in front of it. A larger figure beside a markedly smaller figure, the size of a young child.

"Ben?" she muttered under her breath. Was it her son or some other child? They'd searched a day and a half. This had to be Ben. But if only she could see his face, even his hair, she'd know. "Can we get closer? Look through a window?"

"I don't advise that," Tobias said. "If we were using a Predator, it would be different. We could get a clear visual from a distance. With these smaller drones, it would have to get near a window. We have more than enough to green-light HRT. It'll be their call regarding an actual visual as they close in."

Henry's call.

Allison forced herself to breathe, trying to settle the nerves in her belly.

Tobias got on the phone. "HRT Commander. You're cleared to proceed. We have confirmation of the vehicle in question on-site along with three individuals. One is a child. I repeat. One is a child. You will be patched through to the CBP surveillance post. They'll provide coordinates and await your instructions."

Heart pounding, Allison set her coffee down out of fear she'd drop her cup with the sudden tremble in her hands.

"Roger that," Henry said in a clear, steady voice. "We're wheels up in two minutes."

Chapter Twenty

The six-person team had spent the time waiting to head out quietly reading, contemplating the mission or trying to catch a few futile winks of sleep. Now it was go-time.

Henry gave his directives. "Breach the house. Kill the power. Clear room by room, first floor to second. Neutralize the kidnappers. Secure Ben."

There were curt nods from everyone in the staging area, confirming they knew the plan and what to do. They jogged up the stairs outside to the helicopter on the roof. Already sweating in full tactical gear despite the mild weather, Henry embraced the calm that always stole over him when the team deployed.

They ducked as they approached the spinning rotor blades. Two guys strapped themselves to the external benches on either side of the chopper to ride outside. Henry and the others climbed inside the Bell 407.

Live video stream of the target house came in over Henry's and Valentine's tablets, but all the operators received real-time updates through the earpieces that fit under their sound-deadening hearing protection.

Based on the size of the house from the initial pictures and video, they should be in and out in two min-

utes. But things seldom went without a hitch and they'd
trained for every hiccup imaginable.

The fast and steady helicopter sliced through the cool
night air. They all wore full body armor and helmets
with a thermal monocle affixed on top. The straps of
their M-4 assault rifles were slung over their shoulders,
Glocks with sound suppressors were holstered on their
hips and stun grenades on their utility belts. Valentine
was always ready to rock and roll if they had to use explosive breaching charges.

As they neared the city of Ensenada, the pilots
donned their night-vision goggles, one at a time, giving
each other a minute to adjust. They banked left, looping
in north of the target. At five miles out, they would slow
from 160 mph to 80 mph, drop another hundred feet and
turn off their navigation lights to hide their approach.

"CBP Command, do another sweep of the house,"
Henry instructed Rosalind, "to reaffirm the position of
all three individuals. I'm going to need visual confirmation beyond thermal before we touch down."

He needed to see Ben.

"On it. Sending in Bravo, and Alpha will also be on-
site any minute."

Henry held the monitor tight in his gloved hands.

While he waited, he decided to make sure everyone was thumbs-up all around one last time. "Final
comms check," Henry said to the team through the
voice-activated throat mike. He called off each name
on his team. In return, he received *check*. If anyone had
a last-minute issue, that would have been the chance to
make it known.

CJ came on the line. "When you're ready, toggle to

the file I just sent you. It's a digitized blueprint of what we could make out of the house."

Henry pulled it up. "Got it." Looking across the way, he caught a nod from Valentine that he had received the schematic that was a best guesstimate to reduce the element of surprise. But it wouldn't eliminate it completely.

Anything that prevented them from going in totally blind was a help.

The others were in the zone, prepping for ingress and retrieval. Tense. Determined to do whatever was necessary to extract the hostage.

As team lead, Henry knew every innocent life mattered, each mission carried the same weight.

But he was more than a team lead in this. He was a father, and this was his son. Every person on the chopper knew the stakes were personal.

They were close to the target, but not lights out yet. His men snapped their M-4s up to their shoulders in preparation.

Henry switched back to the livestream video.

The Bravo drone made a pass of the second-floor bedroom, where the lights were on and the only occupants of the house were situated. Hovering in the air, it drew closer to the window. The camera zoomed in on Lourdes, seated in a chair, reading a book.

El Escorpion was on the floor in front of the television, playing a video game. A small figure sat on the other side of him, farther away from the window, but there wasn't a clear visual.

Bravo got closer, changing angles, shifting higher and lower.

Then *El Escorpion* set the game controller down and leaned back, resting on his hands.

Ben's face came up on the screen.

A knot of emotion Henry could barely handle crowded his chest, making it impossible to breathe.

LOURDES LOOKED UP from her book to catch Javier glance out the window for the hundredth time. He was ever watchful since his place in Culiacán had been raided. But this time something caught his attention because he paused the video game.

"Why'd you stop it?" Ben asked, throwing up a hand in frustration. "I was finally winning."

"Give me a minute, little man." His voice lost all softness, taking on a sharp-edged tone.

Setting the controller on the floor, Javier stood and went to the window. Staring at the dark sky, he squinted, his brow creasing.

"What is it?" Lourdes asked.

"See those lights?" He pointed to the sky.

Closing her book, she unfolded her legs and got up, tossing it behind her into the chair.

"Where?" She glanced out the window in the direction he indicated. In the distance, she spotted three lights moving fast through the darkness, one white and two others smaller and blinking red just before they winked out. "What happened to them?"

"They went dark." Javier's body tensed beside her.

"What do you mean? Who? Police?"

"No. Police wouldn't have thought to kill the lights," he said low and calmly. "My guess, it's a tactical unit."

"Maybe they'll pass by," she said. "It doesn't necessarily mean anything. Right?" There had to be more than one criminal keeping a low profile in the middle of nowhere.

"I bet it's my dad," Ben said. "He's a real-life super-hero who saves people. My mom says he's better than Batman because he's not a vigilante."

"What does your father do?" Javier asked, not looking back at Ben, but staring straight ahead at the darkness.

"FBI. Hostage Rescue Team."

A little white machine with small propellers descended in front of the window.

Lourdes leaned in for a closer look. "Are those cameras?"

A second white machine joined the first.

"Drones." Javier swore under his breath as anger flashed across his face. "My boss should've warned me about the father." Then just as quickly a veneer of icy calm settled over him. "We've got four minutes, maybe less, before they get here." He checked his watch and then pulled out his phone. "Go to your room and pack a light bag. Essentials only. Hurry."

A slow pulse of fear throbbed in her veins. "Who are you calling?"

"There are two last-resort measures I've been instructed to execute in the event of something like this. I have to make a call to set one in motion."

"What do you mean *last resort*?"

"That inbound chopper and those drones means it's the end of the line with the kid."

His gaze darted away as he dialed on the cell. "It's me, *El Escorpion*. You need to track someone down. *Y asesinar*." He said the last two words in Spanish. *And assassinate.* "A woman. There in Manhattan." Javier glanced at Lourdes and shooed her away to follow his orders.

Whirling for the hall, she hurried to her room.

She passed the door to her personal panic room and entered the closet. Grabbing a backpack, she frantically looked around. She stuffed a change of clothing into the bag and hustled out. Not bothering with toiletries, she focused on irreplaceable stuff. A thumb drive with pictures of her and Javier and of her students. Her parents' wedding rings. Birth certificate. Passport.

Zipping up the backpack, she ran down the hall back to the guest room.

Javier ended the call, slipped his phone into his pocket and took out his gun. "Head to the entrance to the tunnel and wait for me there while I seal the other entry points."

"Okay." She put a hand on Ben's shoulder, getting up on his feet, to show him the way.

"No." Javier snatched the boy backward by his shirt collar. "He's not going with us."

"Why not?" Maybe her brother had come to his senses and would leave him behind for the rescue team.

"He's the second thing I have to take care of as a last-resort measure."

Her gut filled with ice-cold dread. Shaking her head in confusion, she absorbed the meaning of his words. *Take care of?* Horrified realization dawned on her. "You can't do this. I won't let you."

He took out a silencer and screwed it onto the barrel. "You can't stop me."

Ben lunged for her, throwing his small arms around her waist. "Lola, please don't let him hurt me."

She wrapped her arms around him, holding him close. "I won't leave without him."

"Damn it—"

The sound of the helicopter's powerful thumping rotors drawing near silenced Javier and had him spinning toward the window. "I've got to seal the doors and windows now. I'll leave the entrance to the tunnel open, but if you try to take that kid through, then you'll be forced to watch him die."

Javier bolted from the room, heading for the closest security panel, which was in his room.

Oh, God. She didn't know what to do. But her instincts screamed not to let any harm come to Ben.

The tunnel was a mile long. There was no way she could outrun her brother, especially not with a small child.

There had to be another option. She simply had to figure it out within the next thirty seconds or the child clinging to her would die.

Outside on the lawn, a helicopter touched down a few yards away. Several figures cloaked in black and carrying assault rifles leaped from the aircraft and raced toward the house.

The security protocol engaged with a rumbling noise as the reinforced steel shutters began rolling down over the windows and outer doors.

The rescue team wouldn't make it inside before the house was locked down and Javier would be back any second.

Lourdes grabbed Ben's hand, determined to protect him somehow. Holding him tight, she led him into hall. They rushed down the corridor toward her room.

"Lola!" Javier called as he left his bedroom at the opposite end of the hallway. "What are you doing?"

Lourdes dashed into her room, locked the door and hustled to her security panel. She didn't have the code to halt the lockdown of the house and give the rescue team a chance to get inside, so she did the next best thing. The only thing within her power.

She slapped the *Panic* button, opening the door to the safe room.

It was the one space in the house not linked to the overall security system, which ran independently. A fail-safe Javier had thought of to ensure her protection.

She dragged Ben inside. Motion lights flickered on as she shuffled him behind her.

A heavy thud resounded against her bedroom door, making her jump. There was another boom. Followed by another. Javier was kicking in the door.

She shooed Ben deeper into the room that was the size of a walk-in closet and gestured for him to duck down on the other side of the shelving unit full of supplies.

Quickly, she tapped in her personal code on the panel to lock it. Eight digits she had chosen without Javier's knowledge.

The five-inch hardened steel door began sliding closed. At the same time, her bedroom door burst open, slamming against the wall.

Her throbbing heart flew into her throat as she met Javier's enraged eyes. He charged toward the panic room in a fury as though possessed by the devil.

Just before he reached the threshold, the door sealed shut between them.

"No!" He roared and banged against the thick metal, the violent thuds reverberating through her. "Open it!"

She turned on the intercom. "I can't. I won't let you hurt him."

"Lourdes, we don't have much time. We have to leave."

She looked at the panel of monitors on the wall that provided various views around the perimeter of the house as well as inside.

The rescue team was using a battering ram against the reinforced barricade over the front door. But the shutters had been designed to withstand that very tool because every SWAT team on both sides of the border used them. They'd never get in like that.

"If I open that door," she said, "you'll kill him. He's just a child."

A series of beeps resounded on the other side of the door.

She stared at the monitor showing her room. He was inputting a code, trying to get in.

A buzzer sounded. "Access denied," an automated female voice said.

"You should leave," Lourdes said.

More beeps. "Access denied."

Lourdes gritted her teeth at her brother's tenacity. "You won't guess it." At least, she prayed he wouldn't. "You're only wasting time."

She cringed at the prospect of her brother being arrested, but she'd trade her life for the boy's in a blink.

"Access denied."

"Do you know why I had it configured for eight digits?" Javier asked. "Because I knew you'd choose a date. Day, month, year. Something easy for you to remember. You chose a date, didn't you?"

A chill shot down her spine. She had. But not something he'd readily assume she'd pick because it didn't mark any event in *her* life.

"I'm going to get in and kill that kid," he said. "But

if you open the door now, we still have a chance to get away."

"Go to hell!"

Eight chirps from the system. "Access denied."

Ben jumped up and ran to her.

She wrapped her arms around him and hugged him. "I won't let anything happen to you," she promised.

He shuddered against her. His heart hammered so hard in his chest, she felt it in her stomach.

There was a lot of blood on her brother's hands. Most of the people he'd killed had probably deserved it. Gangsters and drug dealers. Bad people, which had made it easy for her to look the other way. She hated herself for not protecting the nanny, but there was no negotiation, no justification, when it came to a child.

"Access denied."

She watched on the monitor as outside the house, the rescue team abandoned the ram. One man placed wads of a puttylike substance on the four corners of the main shutter. Then he positioned small devices in the center of each. They were going to blow it. Any minute now, they would breach the front door.

"You could never remember Mom's and Dad's birthdays," Javier said. "It's not ours. Not the day they died. Not the day you became a teacher. Or the day that doctor ruined you. I'll figure it out and I'll get in. But it's eating away our time. Just open it!" He banged on the door.

"No. Go, Javier. While you still have a chance."

"Please, Lola, I'm begging you. Open it before it's too late." He pressed his forehead to the door. "You've got to listen to me. I always know best. I'm older."

Older by six minutes. And in most things, she did listen to him, trusted him to guide her. But not in this.

She held Ben tighter. "You can still make it to the tunnel. They'll be distracted with me and getting the boy back. Just leave."

"They'll arrest you. I can't let you go to jail for something I did. Please." There was such desperation, such entreaty, in that last word, it wrenched her heart in two.

"It's okay," she said to Javier, her chest aching. "I don't matter."

"Yes, you do. You matter to me!"

Tears welled in her eyes. "Javier, I love you more than anything in this world. But I won't open it. Leave me and don't look back."

"I can't!" He slapped the door and kicked it.

"Why not?" she asked on a choking sob.

"Because you're the only good thing in my life." His voice was thick with anguish that she felt in the pit of her soul.

If she could've opened that door, she would've, but the cost was too high.

"That's it," Javier said. "I know the code."

Boom!

The house shook under the force of the detonating explosives as the front door was blown.

On the monitor, the rescue team swept inside the house through a cloud of smoke, spread out on the lower level and headed for the stairs.

In her room, Javier lifted his head from the door. "You always put me ahead of yourself the same way I've done with you. The code isn't about you. Is it? It's something to do with me. The only thing that's ever come between us." He raised the back of his hand to the camera.

The scorpion tattoo filled the screen.

Dread gripped her heart in an icy fist. The code was the date he'd become *El Escorpion*.

Eight beeps chimed. "Access granted."

The thick steel door slid open.

"You should've listened to me. I told you I'd get in." Javier swooped inside and snatched Ben from her arms.

They were cornered upstairs in the panic room. There was only one thing her brother could do next to buy time, but it would eventually cost Ben his life. Of that, she was certain.

So she beat her brother to it. She spun and grabbed the first thing her hand reached on the shelving unit inside. Holding a flashlight, she swung at the security panel on the wall and struck it with all her might.

Crack!

The screen shattered into a hundred webbed pieces and the light blinked out.

"No!" Javier growled. "Lourdes, what did you do?"

Now her brother needed Ben alive unless he had a death wish. Going out like a kamikaze wasn't his style. Javier was a survivor.

The lights in the house went out, throwing them into darkness. Heavy footfalls pounded up the steps. Then the backup generator kicked in and amber emergency lights came on.

A string of profanity flew from Javier's mouth. He threw on a bulletproof vest and tossed one her way. "I guess we'll have to do this the hard way."

Chapter Twenty-One

They cleared the room where Ben and his kidnappers had been earlier. With sealed shutters over the windows, the drones' capabilities were limited to thermal imaging.

"We had heat signatures in the last room on the second floor," Rosalind said, "east side of the hall. But they disappeared."

"How?" He gave the hand signal to proceed to the right and check it out.

"I don't know."

"Maybe," CJ said, "their heat signatures are being shielded by something."

"There is a light source emanating from what looks like a dead space," Rosalind said. "We're not getting anything at all from the small area besides the flicker of light around the edges."

Henry was the second man in the line moving down the hall.

"A room with lead walls," CJ said. "Panic room?"

"Then why is the door open, letting out light?" Rosalind asked.

Excellent question. They would have the answer in ten seconds.

Fitzgerald swept across the doorway of a bedroom, over to the other side, and pressed up against the wall.

A quick peek inside told Henry what he needed to know. There was a panic room. Door wide open, for some reason.

Henry raised his hand and gave the three-second countdown with his fingers.

Fitz pulled the pin and tossed the stun grenade inside.

Henry hated the effect the flash-bang would have on his son, but it was a necessary step. Hopefully, they could get to Ben before the kidnappers had a chance to recover and did something foolish.

The grenade went off. Once the shocking bang and bright flash subsided, they swept into the room, M-4s at the ready.

Henry stopped short, surprised by what he saw while the rest of the team rushed in, taking up positions.

El Escorpion wore a bulletproof vest and ear protection. Then he saw Ben. *El Escorpion* had his hand clutched on the back of the boy's neck, holding his son in front of him like a human shield.

Unwavering resolve ran liquid through Henry. He would sooner die, taking that bastard with him, than let anything happen to his son.

There was a black hood over Ben's face and protective muffs over his ears. A woman cowered low behind them.

El Escorpion gestured for Henry to remove his sound-deadening ear protection.

Henry complied.

El Escorpion took his off, as well. "Helmet, too," he said, the suppressor of his gun pressed against the back of Ben's head.

The demand was to level the playing field a little. To give the hit man a clear head shot if he needed to take it.

But Henry knew that if *El Escorpion*'s gun was aimed at him, then it wouldn't be pointed at his son's head and the team would have an opening.

Loosening his chin strap, Henry stayed laser-focused. He slipped the helmet off, letting it hit the floor.

The rest of the team stood steadfast and poised.

"You're all going to back up and let me and my sister out of this room."

Sister?

Henry was glad to have confirmation that the woman was a blood relation. Those bonds were strong. "First, release the boy."

"Nope," *El Escorpion* said, keeping his head low behind Ben. "He comes with us downstairs. I let him go in the kitchen."

Henry shook his head. The only way his son was leaving this room was with him. This had to end here.

"I will shoot him if you don't move!"

"And we'll put a bullet in your head."

"We leave. Then you get the kid." *El Escorpion* jerked Ben, and his son shuddered.

"Daddy? Are you here, Dad?" Ben asked, his voice so brittle that Henry knew his child was crying under that hood.

"I'm here!" he called out loudly, hoping his son could hear him.

Ben reached out for him and Henry's heart twisted in his chest.

El Escorpion yanked Ben backward a step, tightening his grip on his collar. "If you don't move aside and let us out of this room, the first shot goes in the kid's shoulder."

The threat tore at Henry's resolve, but he couldn't allow them to leave that room.

"Just lay down your weapons and let the boy go," Henry said. "No one has to get hurt."

"Someone will get hurt in the next ten seconds if you don't let us out of here!"

The woman jumped up with palms raised and bolted from the panic room. She rushed toward them.

"Lola, no!"

On pure instinct, Henry grabbed her to keep her from getting in the way. He held her while Fitz checked her for weapons, made sure there wasn't an improvised explosive device strapped to her body.

"Threaten to kill me," she said in a low, ragged breath.

What the hell?

Tears streamed down her face. "Please, it's the only way."

Henry put his arm around her throat, released the M-4 and let it dangle from his shoulder, and took out his Glock. "Let him go, or your sister is going to take a bullet."

"Yeah, right," *El Escorpion* said. "You're FBI. You won't shoot an unarmed woman in cold blood."

He was right. Henry wouldn't, but *El Escorpion* couldn't be sure of that.

"Do you think anyone is going to care if a hit man for *Los Chacales* cartel and his sister took bullets to the head?" Henry said loud enough for the other man to hear, but so low he prayed his son didn't catch the words. He tightened his arm around the woman's throat, hoping it would elicit a terrified expression from her.

Alarm washed over *El Escorpion*'s face.

"I may be FBI, but I'm a father first," Henry said. "If killing your sister is what it will take to get my son back, I won't hesitate to pull the trigger. And every man beside me will turn a blind eye."

"Hooah!" Fitz said, helping Henry sell the bluff.

"Javier," Lourdes said. "I don't want anyone else to die. Not Ben. Not you. Not me. Let this father take his son home. Please, Javier. I'm begging you."

Javier shuttered his eyes, bowing his head. Then he shoved Ben out of the panic room and lowered his weapon.

Raising his palms, Javier kneeled on the floor, assuming the position. Fitz cuffed him while Valentine restrained the woman.

Henry dashed forward and scooped his son into his arms, hauling him to the side. He knocked the earmuffs off Ben's head and yanked the hood from his face.

"Daddy!" His little arms flew around Henry's neck.

"I'm here." Choked up, he hugged his son, who clung to him tightly.

"I knew you'd come."

"Of course." He hugged him harder before pulling back and inspecting him to make sure he hadn't been harmed.

As Henry's gloved hands moved over Ben's face, his son said, "I'm okay. Lola kept me safe."

Fitz searched Javier and confiscated a cell phone and switchblade before hauling him out of the room.

"Can I say goodbye?" Lourdes asked.

Ben ran to her and gave her a hug that she couldn't reciprocate. "Thank you for keeping your promise."

She nodded with tears in her eyes. "I'm sorry this happened to you. Good luck next month, on your spelling bee. And take your inhaler from my pocket." While Ben took his inhaler, she looked up at Henry. "The man who ordered Javier to kidnap your son made contact on his cell phone."

Henry put his hand on Ben's shoulder and pulled him back to his side. "We've got it." Standard procedure to search someone. CJ would check the data and run it to ground.

"Not the phone you found in his pocket," she said. "The one he stashed on the second shelf in the panic room."

One of his guys hustled inside the room and rifled through the shelf she'd indicated. "Bingo, boss!"

"Whoever that man is, the leader of *Los Chacales* cartel, he needs to be stopped," she said, and Henry couldn't agree more.

Valentine herded her out of the room.

Henry picked up his son, grateful to have him safe in his arms. So everyone back home was clear, he said over comms, "Hostage is unharmed and secure."

BEN'S SAFE.

Allison repeated the words in her head again, seated in the back of the lead vehicle of the joint FBI/SDPD convoy pulling into the driveway of Vargas's compound.

At last, this nightmare was going to be over and that bastard was going to jail. His reign of terror was at an end. The victory had been hard-won, paid for in blood.

With Tori's life. With her son's abduction. And countless near misses like the explosives in the vans.

They exited the vehicles, a force of twenty strong.

Tobias rounded the hood of the SUV and came up to her. "Like we agreed, you wait here."

She nodded. Tobias had agreed to let her witness the arrest, but since she was emotionally invested, he didn't want her inside the house when it happened. Everything by the book; they weren't going to give Vargas's lawyers any loopholes to exploit.

In the night, the flashing red and blue lights gleaming off the fleet of vehicles was a glorious sight to behold.

The bodyguards were restrained and thrown into the police van.

Then Vargas emerged, hands cuffed behind his back. He was hauled out his front door. On one side of Vargas was Nick. On the other was a man dressed like one of the bodyguards, but who obviously wasn't. She presumed it was Teflon. The insider who'd given the go-ahead to get a warrant.

Immense satisfaction washed over Allison as Vargas was ushered down the steps to an FBI SUV.

Before he was put inside, Allison walked up to him. "You're finally going to get what you deserve."

Vargas laughed. The sound was maniacal, taking her aback. Then his gaze fell to her and the wry humor drained from his face. "You think this is over?"

"Yes. I do." She flashed a confident smile. "You're going away for a very long time."

"I risked everything," Vargas said. "My entire empire. Just to see my daughter one last time, to hold her, kiss her cheek and tell her how much I love her." He clucked his tongue. "The moment your son was retrieved, I knew I'd lose my leverage. Don't you think I planned for this outcome?"

Her skin prickled with warning, but she dismissed it as Vargas messing with her head one last time. "It was a bad gamble on your part and, obviously, you didn't plan well enough."

"I've made you suffer, Marshal. You have paid, not quite as dearly as I wanted." He gave a rueful grin. "I'm done with you and yours, but…" A lopsided grin hitched on his mouth. "The marshals took my daughter and I will have my vengeance. A life for a life."

Whether a threat or a promise, coming from a powerful man with nothing left to lose made it utterly terrifying.

Nick got Vargas loaded in the SUV, went around to the other side and climbed in.

Allison stepped away from the vehicle.

"I'm Special Agent Max Webb," the man beside her said. Also known as Teflon.

She shook his hand. "Deputy Marshal Allison Chen-Boyd."

"I gathered." He glanced at the vehicle Vargas was in. "Don't let him get in your head. He already tried with me. Threatened to have me disemboweled for my treachery."

That wasn't a pleasant image.

Tobias hurried down the front stairs, catching her attention. "They just landed."

Allison's heart leaped with joy. "I'm going to head over."

"One of the officers will take you," Tobias said. "Get you there faster. I cleared it with Captain Roessler."

"Are you heading to the FBI building?" Max asked.

Allison nodded. "Yeah."

"Mind if I ride along? The sooner I reclaim my life, the better."

"Not at all."

Allison and Max climbed into the back of the police cruiser and the officer took off, his lights flashing but the siren muted.

She couldn't wait to see Ben. To hold him.

But Vargas had succeeded in his last taunt. She couldn't stop thinking about it.

"What do you think Vargas meant by a life for a life?" she asked Max. "Did he call anyone? Issue some final order?"

"Not in the past few hours. I've been with him the entire time. But he's a strategic planner. It's possible that he had some fail-safe in place in case they found your son and he was arrested."

Another cold brush in the pit of her stomach. "What kind of fail-safe?"

Max raised his eyebrows, looking weary. "Knowing Vargas, the bad kind where someone ends up dead."

The police cruiser pulled up in front of the FBI building. Henry and Ben were crossing the lobby, headed for the door. Henry had removed his tactical gear, but was still dressed in his black utilitarian clothes, with Ben in his arms.

Never in her life had Allison felt such joy as she did at the sight of her husband carrying Ben outside.

The police car stopped, and anticipation quivered through her. The officer disengaged the locks on the back doors.

She threw open her door and jumped out, making her way to them.

Henry set Ben down on the ground.

Allison ran to her son as fast as she could. Ben lunged for her, and she caught him in her arms.

"Mommy! I missed you."

"I missed you, too, munchkin." She kissed his cheek, ran her hand through his hair, and kissed him again and again. "So much, baby."

A rolling rush of emotions inundated her. She buried her face in his neck, crying tears of relief and happiness. Henry wrapped his arms around them both in a bear hug.

She'd come so close to losing them. But now she had them both in her arms and she was never letting go. Of Ben. Or Henry.

This was her family and she was going to hold it, no matter what.

Epilogue

The next day, they sat at the table in their hotel suite, eating room service.

They'd gotten back to the hotel late last night. Adrenaline had kept them all up for hours.

Ben had slept in the bed with them and Sprocket. Surprisingly, her son didn't have any nightmares, but Allison knew that he still might, especially once they went back to the house where Ben had been abducted.

Tobias was making sure all listening devices had been removed before they returned home. She wasn't in any rush.

"Can I have another slice of pizza?" Ben, still in his pajamas despite the fact it was now early evening, asked with a smile.

Allison took one from her plate and put it on his.

They'd ordered room service for brunch and half the menu later for dinner. There was a variety of options to choose from, but if her son wanted more pizza, then he'd have it. She didn't care what she ate. She just wanted to stay in this little bubble with Ben and Henry for as long as possible.

"Fries, too, please?" Ben asked.

Henry laughed and gave him extra.

"Is it too late for you to accept that position in Quantico?" Allison asked Henry.

His eyes lit up. "No, it's not, but are you sure?"

"I think a change might be good for all of us." She loved San Diego and the easy flight up to San Fran to visit her parents, but Vargas had ruined this place for her. A darkness overshadowed it like a pall.

Not to mention, every time she set foot in that house, she'd think back to the day Ben had been snatched from them. Used like a pawn in one man's sick, twisted game of revenge.

Moving wouldn't be a sacrifice. She could do her job in Virginia just as easily as she had in San Diego, but Quantico was the only place Henry could advance. Relocating would be best for their family.

"Ally, hon, are you saying—"

"I'm saying that you're stuck with me." She smiled at Ben and ruffled his hair.

"There's no one else I'd rather be stuck with. Do you know that?"

Taking Henry's hand in hers, she did know that.

They'd make the move like they'd discussed before, see a counselor to work through their issues while they transitioned, and take care of their son. Get him into therapy and make sure he knew how much he was loved.

"Daddy, did your team save the woman, too?" Ben wiped syrup from his mouth with the back of his hand.

Woman? "Sweetie, we explained about Tori. Unfortunately, no one could rescue her."

Ben frowned. "I don't mean Tori."

"Lourdes is in jail," Henry said gently. "I know you think she was your friend, but she did a bad thing and has to pay for that."

"I'm not talking about her, either," Ben said. "I mean the woman in Manhattan."

"Manhattan, sweetie? What?" Allison looked to Henry for any clarification and he shrugged, looking just as perplexed as she felt.

"Javier called someone right before Daddy came and got me. He told the person on the phone to track down a woman in Manhattan. Then he said '*asesinar*.' I know that means assassin or assassinate." Ben looked at Henry. "That woman, Daddy. Did you save her, too, and keep the bad men from getting her?"

Allison's skin prickled.

The marshals took my daughter and I will have my vengeance. A life for a life.

Who in the hell did Vargas want to kill that was in Manhattan?

"Munchkin, did Javier say a name?"

Ben nodded. "Wendy somebody."

She exchanged a glance with Henry. "I don't know any Wendy."

"Javier hasn't been cooperative in custody," Henry said. "I can ask Tobias to have someone question the sister, Lourdes. Maybe she'll give us the name."

"Lourdes left the room," Ben said, "while Javier was on the phone."

"Munchkin, can you think back and try to remember what her last name is?" Allison asked.

"It's really important, Ben. We can't help her if we don't know who she is," Henry said.

"Her last name sounded like the name of the ice-cream shop."

"You mean the name of the gelato place?" Allison asked.

Ben shook his head. "The one in the mall. Her last name sounded like Häagen-Dazs."

Allison's blood ran cold, but her head was clear. "Haas? Was the name Haas?"

"That's it," Ben said brightly.

"Wendy Haas. She must be someone close to Dutch. He mentioned a sister once." Then it made sense. The one person Vargas would want to hurt more than Allison or Draper was the man who'd stolen his daughter's heart. Dutch Haas. "She'll be an unsuspecting target."

Allison stood and grabbed her purse. Digging around inside, she tried to find her phone.

Henry was out of his chair, crossing the room. A second later, he was beside her with her cell phone. He pressed a steady palm to her cheek. "We'll divide and conquer. You contact Draper and have him dig up a phone number and address on Wendy. I'll call Eielson Air Base and leave a message. As soon as Dutch and Isabel get back, he'll know."

She gave a curt nod that said all the things she didn't have time to voice. *Thank you. I'm glad we're a team again. We're better together than apart. I love you.*

He pressed his lips to hers, quick and light, and the kiss told her what she already knew in her heart. They were in this, like everything else, together.

* * * * *

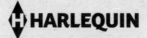

The narrow mountain road ended at the edge of a rock cliff. It wasn't as if Ford Cardwell had forgotten that. No, when he saw where he was, he knew it was why he'd taken this road and why he was going so fast as he approached the sheer vertical drop to the rocks far below. It would have been so easy to keep going, to put everything behind him, to no longer feel pain.

Pine trees blurred past as the pickup roared down the dirt road to the nothingness ahead. All he could see was sky and more mountains off in the distance. Welcome back to Montana. He'd thought coming home would help. He'd thought he could forget everything and go back to being the man he'd been.

His heart thundered as he saw the end of the road coming up quickly. Too quickly. It was now or never.

The words sounded in his ears, his own when he was young. He saw himself standing in the barn loft looking out at the long drop to the pile of hay below. Jump or not jump. It was now or never.

He was within yards of the cliff when his cell phone rang. He slammed on his brakes. An impulsive reaction to the ringing in his pocket? Or an instinctive desire to go on living?

The pickup slid to a dust-boiling stop, his front tires just inches from the end of the road. Heart in his throat, he looked out at the plunging drop in front of him.

His heart pounded harder. Just a few more moments—a few more inches—and he wouldn't have been able to stop in time.

His phone rang again. A sign? Or just a coincidence? He put the pickup in Reverse a little too hard and hit the gas pedal. The front tires were so close to the edge that for a moment he thought the tires wouldn't have purchase. Fishtailing backward, the truck spun away from the precipice.

Ford shifted into Park and, hands shaking, pulled out his still-ringing phone. As he did, he had a stray thought. How rare it used to be to get cell phone coverage here in the Gallatin Canyon of all places. Only a few years ago the call wouldn't have gone through.

Without checking to see who was calling, he answered it, his hand shaking as he did. He'd come so close to going over the cliff. Until the call had saved him.

"Hello?" He could hear noises in the background. *"Hello?"* He let out a bitter chuckle. A robocall had saved him at the last moment, he thought, chuckling to himself.

But his laughter died as he heard a bloodcurdling scream coming from his phone.

Don't miss
Trouble in Big Timber *by B.J. Daniels,*
available June 2021 wherever
Harlequin Intrigue books and ebooks are sold.

Harlequin.com

HIEXP0521